PETER PAN
the motion picture event
The novelisation of the hit movie

By Alice Alfonsi
Based on the motion picture screenplay by
P.J. Hogan and Michael Goldenberg
Based upon the Original Stageplay and Books written by
J.M. Barrie

London   New York   Sydney

First published in Great Britain by Pocket Books
An imprint of Simon & Schuster UK Ltd, a Viacom company
Africa House, 64–78 Kingsway, London WC2B 6AH

POCKET BOOKS and colophon are registered trademarks of Simon & Schuster
A CIP catalogue record for this book is available from the British Library.

ISBN 07434 7802 9

1 3 5 7 9 10 8 6 4 2

Printed and bound in Great Britain by Cox & Wyman Ltd, Reading, Berkshire

www.simonsays.co.uk
www.peterpanmovie.net

PETER PAN

the motion picture event

The novelisation of
the hit movie

Contents

1

The Happy Home

"All children grow up. Except one."

The strange whispering thought disturbed Wendy Moira Angela Darling, who was almost thirteen. With a frown, she brushed away a stray lock of long brown hair. But she could not brush away the whispering thought. And, for a moment, she lost all powers of concentration.

Why should such a thought pop into her head, wondered Wendy. It had *nothing* to do with the story she was telling her two little brothers and their nursemaid, a big St. Bernard dog named Nana. What did "growing up" have to do with evil pirates and a clever princess, anyway?

A vision pressed itself upon Wendy, too, along with the whispering thought. She saw a strange forest, dark and deep and wild.

Now what business did a savage wilderness have appearing to her in a nursery, in a London townhouse, in the civilised year of 1895? Unless, of course, the forest was the setting for some grand *new* story, Wendy thought, a story like the one she was in the middle of telling right now.

"Tell us more, Wendy," Michael, cried. "Finish the story, please."

Michael was Wendy's youngest brother. He was eight years old, had a freckled face and adored her nightly tales of forgetful kings and kindly dragons, of orphaned wolves, enchanted castles, princes, gnomes and evil queens. At his request, Wendy gathered her thoughts and continued this evening's story where she'd left off.

"As Cinderella stepped from the golden carriage," said Wendy, "she found herself most impertinently surrounded by evil pirates!"

"Pirates?" said John doubtfully. John was Wendy's other brother. He was eleven, wore small round spectacles, and was at times quite serious about things.

"Why, John!" Wendy cried. "Don't you believe in pirates?"

John nodded. "Rather!" he declared. After all, he thought, whether he believed in them or not, who wouldn't want to hear a good story about pirates?

"And pirates would make this story more exciting, too," said little Michael.

"Then pirates we shall have," Wendy replied. "A whole bunch of them!"

The boys applauded. Nana, wearing a lacy white nursemaid's cap on her big, furry head, barked once.

"There was the pirate Cecco, who cut his name on the back of the governor of the prison at Goa," Wendy continued. "And Bill Jukes, every inch of him tattooed. And Noodler, whose hands were fixed on backwards."

"Ooooooeerrrr!" howled John and Michael in gleeful disgust.

"And then there was the cruellest pirate of all . . ." Wendy paused.

John's eyes widened behind his round spectacles. Little Michael's freckled face grew pale.

"It was *Captain Hook*!" Wendy cried. "With eyes as blue as forget-me-nots, save when he claws your belly with the iron hook he has instead of a right hand. Then his eyes turn ghastly *red*. 'Girlie,' said Captain Hook. 'We come for ye glass slippers!'"

Wendy jumped to her feet and put her hands on her hips.

"Why you thundering curmudgeon," Wendy said, mimicking the scolding voice of an outraged Cinderella. "Who be you to order me about and call me 'girlie?'"

As she spoke, John jumped past a table crowded with toy soldiers and plucked a wooden sword from his toy box.

"Then Hook unsheathed his cutlass!" John announced, playing the part of the pirate captain. He waved the wooden sword menacingly then placed its blunt tip under his sister's chin, sure she would surrender.

But no!

"The brave English girl boldly met the pirate's gaze," Wendy declared. "'Sir, I am a Lady, and the tip of my sword—'"

"Your *sword*?" cried John, perplexed.

Wendy produced her own wooden blade.

"'*My* sword,'" she said triumphantly. "'Granted me by my fairy godmother! And with my sword, I will soon teach you some manners.'"

With that, Wendy knocked the toy sword out of her brother's hand. John jumped away, ducking under a table to make his escape. Wendy was on his heels.

"Oh, Wendy," gushed Michael. "You tell the best, best, bestest stories!"

Michael, John and Wendy were having so much fun, they barely noticed Nana's paws clicking across the hardwood floor. Something had caught the dog's attention – a shadowy figure appeared to be listening at the window.

"Run, pirate!" cried Wendy in the meantime, chasing John around the nursery.

"What happened then?" cried little Michael. "Do stop fighting and tell!"

Wendy leaped onto the bed and jumped up and down.

"As Hook came at her, Cinderella flung herself down in front of him so cleverly that he took a header right over her and impaled himself upon his own iron hook!" said Wendy breathlessly.

Pretending to be Hook, John clutched his tummy and plunged to the floor. Wendy stood over him and formed the shape of a gun with her fingers and thumb.

"And before Hook could rise again, the brave Cinderella settled the matter once and for all with her revolver—"

"Her *revolver*?" John cried. "Where did Cinderella get—"

Suddenly, Nana barked. The children looked up. The big dog had parted the white lacy curtains with her wet nose. A sparkling ball of light glowed brilliantly in the chilly darkness. For a moment, the glow illuminated two shining eyes. Someone was spying on them through the window! But how could that be when the window was three floors up?

Wendy, John and Michael raced across the room. But the fairy light vanished as suddenly as it had appeared. Now the only lights they saw were the flickering lamps of London shining far below them in the chilly dark.

Just then, the cuckoo clock on the mantle struck six. Time to get ready for dinner!

"I won't be bathed!" Michael cried, running away from Nana, who barked and tried to steer him into the bathroom. "I won't go, I won't!"

"Two minutes more," John pleaded. "One minute more?"

But Nana would not be swayed.

Wendy remained at the window, staring into the darkness. It was then that she noticed a leaf on the window sill. It was a leaf too strange to have come from any tree in England. She peered at the skeleton leaf by the light of the moon.

Strange indeed, that leaf. Of course, what troubles a grown-up will never trouble a child. (For instance, a child may remember to mention, years after it happened, that he once met a ghost and had a lovely game with it!)

Wendy, instead of worrying about where the leaf came from, or saving it to analyse and be bothered about later, simply released it. A breeze snatched it from her fingers, and the leaf spiralled up into the night.

Above Wendy, on the rooftop of the townhouse, the shadowy figure watched the girl's head pop back inside the nursery window. As the strange leaf rose on the wind, the figure reached out a hand and snatched it back.

Nana, meanwhile, had her paws full trying to get the boys bathed for the evening.

"I will not be bathed!" howled Michael like a wild Indian. He resembled one, too. Michael wore nothing more than a feathered headdress as he scurried around the nursery!

Finally, Nana gave up. She left the nursery and trotted down the hallway.

"Hah!" Michael snorted, waving his arm victoriously.

Suddenly Nana turned. Head held low, the dog charged the boy. Michael screamed. Then he turned to run.

Too late!

Nana quickly caught up with the boy. Ducking her head, Nana flipped Michael onto her back. Then, still running, Nana rushed through the bathroom door and dumped Michael with a great splash into a tub full of steaming water!

"Not fair!" Michael spat, gasping.

But Nana quickly licked Michael's face and all was forgiven. The boy tightly hugged the dog's neck.

Downstairs in the drawing room, the chandelier swayed over the heads of Wendy's father and mother. From upstairs came a crash, then a splash, then the sound of John and Michael laughing.

"Bath time," Mrs Darling said, smiling.

Wendy's mother was the sweetest, most gentle lady in all of London, with a mouth that found something to laugh about every day. Although Mrs Darling gave out many kisses to her husband and children, Wendy believed there was one kiss on her mother's mouth that none of them could ever get. (And there the kiss sat, where everyone could see it!)

Wendy's father was a hard-working man who seemed to know all about the world of business. Of course, the children didn't know about these matters, but Mr Darling often spoke about loans and interest and annuities in a way that would make anyone think well of him.

On this particular evening, Aunt Millicent was joining the family for dinner. The commotion upstairs made her shift in her seat by the fireplace and sigh in a way that made Mr and Mrs Darling uneasy.

"Dear ones," Aunt Millicent began, "there has been talk . . ."

Mrs Darling raised her eyebrow. Aunt Millicent was a kind woman, but she had a passion for being exactly like her neighbours.

Aunt Millicent continued. "It is said that in the basement of Miss Fulson's School, where the nurses wait for their charges, the Darling nurse lays on the *floor*."

"But that is the only difference," Mrs Darling replied.

"George," said Aunt Millicent, appealing to Mr

Darling. "You must consider your position at the bank. A dog for a nurse?"

"George," Mrs Darling said. "Nana is a treasure."

"No doubt," said Mr Darling with a frown. "But I sometimes have an uneasy feeling that Nana . . . does not admire me."

"Oh, no, George," Mrs Darling replied. "I know Nana admires you tremendously . . . and she is cheap!"

Mr Darling smiled, confident that there was never a happier, simpler family anywhere else in the whole world.

2

The Shadow

When dinner was over, the Darlings retired to the drawing room, where Mr Darling entertained his family with a song and Mrs Darling accompanied him on the piano. Little Michael grinned from ear to ear as he watched Wendy dance with John.

His brother looked impressive in his dark blue military jacket. The jacket had a big bright medal with lots of ribbons pinned to its spotless white lapel. On his head John wore a big, triangular hat. He looked quite like his idol, Emperor Napoleon Bonaparte of France.

While the Darlings danced and sang, Aunt

Millicent sat in her rocking chair knitting. Once in a while, she cast suspicious glances at Nana. The dog was sound asleep, tucked in nice and cosy near the fireplace.

Finally the song ended, and Wendy and John fell down onto the sofa, tired and happy.

"Wendy's turn!" Michael cried.

John nodded. "Wendy *must* tell us a story."

"Tell us of Cecco," said Michael. "Who carved his name on the Governor at Goa!"

"And Noodler, with his hands on backwards," said John.

Aunt Millicent was appalled. "Good heavens," she cried, throwing up her hands.

"And Hook!" Michael said triumphantly.

"Hook?" said Aunt Millicent, perplexed.

"Hook!" said John gleefully. "A pirate whose eyes turn red as he guts you."

"Upon my soul, such stories," Aunt Millicent said. "It's a disgrace how children are educated nowadays!"

"I am afraid I am not learned at all, Aunt," Wendy explained. "But I do know a thing or two about pirates. My ambition is to write a great novel in three parts about my adventures."

Aunt Millicent blinked. "What adventures?"

"I have yet to have them," Wendy said with a sigh. "But they will be perfectly thrilling when I do."

Aunt Millicent stroked Wendy's hair. "But child," she cooed. "Novelists are not highly thought of in good society, and lady novelists are not thought of at all. And there is nothing so difficult to marry as a novelist."

It was Wendy's turn to be perplexed. "Marry?"

"Aunt Millicent!" Mrs Darling protested. Wendy is not yet thirteen."

"Yet look at her!" Aunt Millicent cried. "Wendy possesses a woman's chin."

Everyone looked at Wendy's chin.

"And had you not noticed?" continued Aunt Millicent. "Observe her mouth."

Everyone peered at Wendy's mouth.

"There, hidden in the right hand corner of Wendy's mouth . . . Is that a kiss I see?"

"A kiss," Michael whispered to John, who nodded.

"Like Mother's kiss," he said.

"The special kiss we cannot get," Michael said.

"A hidden kiss," said Aunt Millicent. "But perfectly conspicuous for those with eyes to see. And it is a special person who sees that kiss."

"What is it for?" Wendy asked softly.

Aunt Millicent smiled. "It is for the greatest adventure of all. They that find it have slipped in and out of heaven."

"Find what?" said Wendy.

"The one the kiss belongs to," Aunt Millicent replied, her eyes suddenly sad. "The special person made especially for you."

Mrs Darling rose and shooed Nana and the children up to the nursery. But the boys disobeyed. Instead of going to their room, they lurked on the stairs, listening to their parents.

"My Wendy, a woman?" sighed Mr Darling. "And so soon."

"*Almost* a woman," Aunt Millicent corrected him. "She must spend less time with her brothers and more time with me. And she must leave the nursery and be given a room of her own!"

At that, John and Michael gasped.

"No adventures," Michael whined.

"No pirates," sighed John.

"No Wendy," they both cried together.

"And George," Aunt Millicent continued. "The daughter of a clerk cannot hope to marry as well as that of a manager. You must make small talk with your superiors at the bank. Get noticed. Be witty. Wit is very fashionable at the moment."

George nodded. Like any good father, Mr Darling would try anything to help Wendy find happiness.

Later that night, in the nursery, Wendy lay in bed. Depressed, she stared at the dark ceiling. "It is the end of me," she said. "My Waterloo."

"Never!" said John from across the room. "They said *almost* a woman. Remember the lady friend of Mother's who was twenty-nine for ten years. If she can do it . . ."

"I can do it!" said Wendy, feeling better already. Then she was quiet a moment. "But how?" she wondered.

John didn't have an answer, and Michael was already asleep. Soon, Wendy was sleeping, too.

Pale moonlight streamed through the curtains, and a light breeze stirred the air.

As a lock of her hair slid across her cheek, Wendy woke. A moment later, her eyes went wide with shock, and she stifled a scream.

Impossibly, the face of a young boy hovered over her head! The boy, who appeared equally startled, sprang weightlessly across the room. At the window, he paused, locking eyes with Wendy.

Suddenly, Nana burst out of her kennel and sprang at the ghostly figure. The dog's teeth missed the boy but caught the edge of the boy's shadow. Stubbornly, Nana dug her claws into the floor and tugged. The strange flying boy was being dragged back into the nursery. Suddenly, there was a tearing sound, and the window slammed shut.

Nana barked as Wendy rushed to the window. But the boy had vanished. Where had he gone? Wendy wondered. Had he fallen?

She ran out of the nursery and into the hallway.

A heavy chest of drawers sat filled with household items. She pulled open a drawer, snatched up a candle, and hurried for the stairs.

Barking, Nana burst into the hallway, still trying to catch the boy's flying shadow. Slowly, the shadow slithered down the wall. When it leaped into the drawer that Wendy had left open, Nana dived forward. Striking the drawer with her paws, she slammed it shut, trapping the mysterious shadow inside.

Meanwhile, Wendy had lit the candle and was hurrying out of the front door. She searched the street for the boy who had flown through her window. But there was no body, for no one had fallen.

Then Wendy looked up. The nursery window was thirty feet above the ground. If the boy hadn't fallen, where had he gone? she wondered. Could he have simply flown away?

Suddenly, she glimpsed something far beyond the nursery window – as far away as anyone might imagine. It appeared like a streak of fire in the night sky, a flash as fleeting as a shooting star.

*

At school the next day, all Wendy could think about was the strange vision of the night before. Was the ghostly boy real? Did he really visit her? Or was it all just a dream?

Art class at Miss Fulsom's School for Girls was to be taken very seriously. All the girls were expected to use their time creatively. Some girls worked on needlepoint. Others painted pictures or arranged flowers.

Wendy, meanwhile, drew a picture. It was the picture of a girl lying in bed. Above her, a boy floated.

"If this is you in bed, then who is this?" Miss Fulsom demanded.

"A boy," Wendy replied.

"Young lady!" Miss Fulsom cried. "I must report this to your parents at once!"

A few minutes later, Wendy watched in horror as Miss Fulsom handed a messenger boy a letter addressed to Mr Darling at the bank. Wendy knew she would be in trouble as soon as her father received that letter from her teacher.

*

Later that day, as Nana escorted John, Michael, and Wendy home from school, Wendy spied a familiar face – the messenger boy! The boy was peddling a bicycle down the street towards Mr Darling's bank.

"Wait!" cried Wendy. "Stop!"

But the messenger boy peddled on. He had an important message to deliver to a Mr Darling at the Fidelity Bank and Assurance Company. He would let no one distract him!

At that same moment, inside the bank, Mr Darling was about to speak to his superior. Sir Edward Quiller-Couch, the president of the company, was a sour man, but he did like it when his underlings made "small talk" and said witty things. For that reason, Mr Darling had been practising his "small talk" all afternoon. Now he was about to take Aunt Millicent's advice and make an effort to make small talk with Sir Edward.

"I advise refusal of this loan, sir," said Mr Darling, handing Sir Edward a letter. "It seems to me that Lord Caversham lives entirely for pleasure."

Sir Edward scrutinised the letter. "How should a peer of the realm live?" he asked.

"For the approbation of his creditors, Sir," Mr Darling replied.

To Mr Darling's delight, Sir Edward roared with laughter.

"Well said, young fellow!" Sir Edward cried. "I shall refuse this loan, and keep an eye on you."

Still smiling, Sir Edward clapped his hand on Mr Darling's shoulder. "And what is your name?"

Before Mr Darling could reply, a worried voice interrupted them.

"Father, I can explain!" Wendy cried, rushing across the marble floor of the bank. She was desperately trying to block the messenger, but the darned boy was determined. He kept right on coming!

Nana burst into the bank a moment later, chasing Wendy. Once inside, the dog tried to slow down, but the floor was too slippery, and Nana skidded right into Wendy.

"Whoa!" Wendy cried, flipping onto Nana's broad back.

The dog kept spinning across the slippery floor, taking Wendy with her as she crashed into Mr Darling and Sir Edward. The two went flying through the air like bowling pins. And Nana kept going, sliding into managers and clerks and even a few customers.

Soon the shiny marble floor of the Fidelity Bank and Assurance Company was littered with fallen bodies, all struggling to rise. And all angry.

"I'm sorry, Father," Wendy sobbed.

But Mr Darling was much too angry to listen.

That night, Mr Darling stripped off Nana's maid's cap and took the dog outside to the dog house.

"I need a nurse," Mr Darling said with a heavy heart, "not a dog."

Then he turned to face his daughter Wendy.

"Wendy," Mr Darling said gently. "Tomorrow you begin instructions on how to become a proper Lady with your Aunt Millicent!"

3

Peter Breaks Through

That night, a gloomy silence hung over the nursery. Mrs Darling struck a match and lit a candle, a night-light for the children.

The boys watched as their mother placed a filigreed glass over the candle, then crossed the room to light a second.

Mrs Darling was dressed for a special evening. Her pink-coloured silk gown and long white opera gloves made her look like a princess as she swept across the nursery floor.

Outside, in the cold, Nana barked continuously.

"She sounds awfully unhappy," Michael said, who felt awfully unhappy himself.

"That is not her unhappy bark," John countered. "That's her bark when she smells danger."

As Michael shivered under his blanket, Mrs Darling tested the window latch to make sure it was locked tight. Then she lit a third candle.

"Mama," Michael said, his voice a whisper. "Can anything harm us after the night-lights are lit?"

Mrs Darling smiled and shook her head. "No, precious. They are the eyes a mother leaves behind to guard her children."

And yet Mrs Darling could not shake a private feeling of worry. She was sorry Mr Darling had put Nana outside, and she didn't like leaving her children. But tonight's party was important for Mr Darling's career.

To calm her nameless fears, Mrs Darling sat down on the edge of Wendy's bed. She stroked her daughter's hair.

"Must you go to the party?" Wendy asked.

Mrs Darling nodded. "Your father is a brave

man, but he will need the 'special kiss' before he can face his colleagues after what happened at the bank today."

"Father? Brave?" said John, who only thought soldiers like Napoleon were truly brave.

Mrs Darling nodded again. "There are different kinds of bravery, John.

"There is the bravery of thinking of others before oneself. Your father has never brandished a sword or fired a pistol – thank heavens! – but he has made many sacrifices for his family and put away many dreams."

"Where did he put them?" Michael asked.

Mrs Darling smiled. "In a drawer. And sometimes, late at night, we take them out and admire them. It gets harder and harder to close that drawer, but he does. And that is why your father is truly brave."

Just then, the nursery door swung open. There stood Mr Darling. He wore evening clothes, a top hat and tails. Behind him stood Aunt Millicent, looking stern. She would be the children's baby-sitter for the evening.

"It is snowing," Mr Darling announced. "We shall catch our death if we go to the party."

"But we *must* go," said Mrs Darling.

"Yes," Aunt Millicent said with a wave of her hand. "Better death than gossip."

And so, Mr and Mrs Darling were off to the party. Not long after they were gone, Michael and John heard a noise. It came from the drawer in the hallway chest, the one that held the trapped shadow. That drawer was now rattling.

"Listen," whispered Michael. "It's Father's dreams . . ."

Soon the rattling slowed, then stopped. In the silence that followed, Wendy and her brothers drifted off to sleep.

High above the Darling home, in a sky sprinkled with stars, the points of light winked softly, as if gossiping about what would happen next. In fact, the stars seemed so close that night, they might have been heaven's spies, watching and waiting for the grown-ups to leave. And when Mr and Mrs Darling did leave, and the children were finally fast asleep, the sky itself seemed to whisper, *It's time, Peter. Go!*

Inside the nursery, the night-lights blinked three times, as if by magic. Then they all went out, and the nursery was plunged into darkness. Silently, the latch on the window began to turn. Then the window slid open. A cool breeze touched Wendy's face, and she smiled in her sleep.

Suddenly, a ball of golden light, no bigger than a fist but a thousand times brighter than the night-lights, burst into the room. Like a living thing, it hurled itself to and fro, casting wild shadows on the walls.

It darted under Wendy's bed, and then streaked towards a corner. Rummaging through John's toy box, the light scattered tin soldiers and little cannons all over the floor.

Then the creature raced through the innards of the huge grandfather clock. Bells tinkled, and the face of the old clock glowed with an eerie light.

Meanwhile, in the hallway, the drawer began to

rattle again. At the sound, the ball of light whisked out of the clock and knocked over a statue of Napoleon.

The crash startled Wendy awake.

Noticing the girl stir, the ball of light settled on top of one of the night-lights, dimming its glow to perfectly mimic the candle flame. Wendy stared at the light. Remembering how her mother had lit the flame, she felt comforted and fell back into a deep sleep.

Through the filigreed glass of the night-light, a tiny face peered at the sleeping Wendy. Then, on fairy wings, Tinker Bell flew out of the nursery and into the hallway. She hovered next to the chest of drawers and peeked through the keyhole. The shadow was still inside the drawer . . . trapped.

Meanwhile, inside the nursery, someone was climbing through the open window. Two bare feet padded quietly across the floor. The feet belonged to the flying boy whom Wendy had seen the night before, when she thought she'd been dreaming.

But Wendy hadn't been dreaming, after all.

Now the boy had returned. He was looking for something he'd lost.

Peter Pan was looking for his shadow.

When Tinker Bell saw Peter, she raced to his side. She flitted around the boy, and he lifted into the air as effortlessly as a butterfly. Then Peter and Tink floated over to the chest of drawers.

When Peter opened the drawer, his shadow popped out. It shook out its arms and legs and stretched, free at last!

Tink rushed the shadow, pushing it towards Peter. But as she got closer to the drawer, Peter's foot accidently closed the drawer, trapping the fairy inside!

Peter pounced on his shadow and wrestled with it up and down the hallway and into the nursery. Finally, he pinned it to the floor with a heavy book end.

The shadow struggled but could not get free. Peter stood over it. Then he sat down and tried to put his shadow on feet first – as if it were a sock. When that didn't work, Peter licked the end of the shadow. Again he failed.

In despair, Peter slumped forward and sobbed.

"Boy, why are you crying?" asked Wendy, who had been awakened by all the commotion.

At the sound of her voice, Peter shot high in the air until he touched the ceiling.

"You can fly!" Wendy exclaimed.

Cautiously, Peter floated back to the floor and landed in front of Wendy. Then he bowed graciously. Thrilled, Wendy bowed, too. Then she studied the strange boy who had entered Wendy's world.

From the golden curls that crowned his head to the strange carved wooden pan pipes he wore slung to his hips with a leather string, Wendy was sure Peter was unlike any boy she'd ever seen. His clothes were made from jungle leaves, bark and feathers, all patched together with the juices that ooze out of trees. But it was the boy's bluer-than-blue eyes that seemed to hold the greatest mystery for Wendy.

Who is this strange, lost, sad little boy? she wondered.

"What is your name?" she asked.

"What is *your* name?" Peter replied.

"I'm Wendy Moira Angela Darling," she said primly.

"I'm Peter . . ." he said in return, pausing a moment as he suddenly realised how brief his name was. "Peter Pan."

"Is that all?" asked Wendy.

Peter nodded.

"Where do you live?" asked Wendy.

"Follow the stars . . . second to the right," said Peter, "and then straight on until morning."

Wendy blinked in surprise. Peter said the words as if he were giving out an address in Piccadilly Circus!

"They put that on letters?" asked Wendy.

Peter Pan shook his head. "Don't get any letters."

"But your mother gets letters."

Peter shrugged. "Don't have a mother."

Wendy was stunned. "No wonder you were crying," she said.

Peter puffed out his chest. "I wasn't crying about mothers," he said defiantly. "I was crying because I can't get my shadow to stick . . . And I wasn't really crying, either!"

Wendy stepped closer to Peter. He backed away from her, frightened. So Wendy turned her attention to the shadow pinned to the floor.

Gingerly, she picked up the shadow's foot, not at all surprised that it was feather-light and cottony to the touch. The shadow suddenly pulled away from Wendy, too.

"Excuse me," Wendy said to the shadow in a soothing voice. Then she turned to Peter.

"I could sew it on for you," she suggested.

While her brothers continued to sleep, Wendy found her sewing kit. She opened the wicker basket and drew out a needle and some black thread.

"This may hurt a little," she cautioned Peter. The boy shrugged indifferently. But his eyes widened a little when he saw the sharp tip of the silver needle.

As Wendy sewed, Tinker Bell beat her fairy wings madly. Tink was furious that Peter was even *talking* to Wendy.

Finally, Wendy finished. She bit off the end of

the thread and tied it. Peter Pan lifted one foot, then another. Each time the shadow obediently followed his master's lead like any normal, well-behaved shadow.

"Oh, the cleverness of me!" crowed Peter.

Wendy raised an eyebrow. "Of course, I did nothing."

"Wendy," Peter Pan purred in an admiring voice. "One girl is worth more than *twenty* boys."

Wendy smiled. "You really think so?"

Peter put his hands on his hips. "I live with boys," he smiled. "The Lost Boys. They are well named."

"Who are they?" Wendy asked.

"Children who fall out of their prams when the nurse is not looking. If they are not claimed in seven days they are sent to the Neverland," he explained. "I'm captain!"

Wendy was amazed. "Are there girls too?"

Peter shook his head. "Girls are much too clever to fall out of their prams."

Wendy liked this boy! "Peter, it is perfectly lovely the way you talk about girls," she said. "I should like to give you a kiss."

Inside the drawer, Tinker Bell heard the word "kiss" and got very upset. She began to bang on the drawer so hard the entire chest shook.

Peter Pan smiled and held out his hand, palm up, waiting for Wendy to give him a kiss.

Wendy sighed. "Don't you know what a kiss is?

"I shall know when you give me one!" Peter said, peeved.

Suddenly, Wendy didn't want to kiss Peter any more. But she didn't wish to hurt his feelings, so she handed him a thimble.

Peter studied the thimble for a few seconds. "I suppose I'm to give you one now," he said with a sigh.

"If you like," Wendy said coyly. She inclined her head towards him and closed her eyes.

Peter found an acorn in his leafy clothes and presented it to Wendy.

"Thank you," Wendy said sincerely. She raced to her jewellery box and dug out a long, thin chain. She attached the acorn to the chain and placed it around her long, delicate neck.

Inside the drawer, Tinker Bell thumped with fury. Trapped inside the chest was one unhappy fairy!

4

Come Away, Come Away!

By the flickering glow of the nursery's night-lights, Wendy studied Peter Pan – a boy who claimed to be the captain of a place called Neverland.

"How old are you, Peter?" Wendy asked.

"Quite young," said Peter, with a wave of his hand.

"Don't you know?"

Peter put a finger under his chin thoughtfully.

"One night I heard Mother and Father talking of what I was to be when I became a man," he said.

Peter's words sounded all too familiar to Wendy.

She caught her reflection in the mirror, her "woman's chin" and shifted unhappily.

"But I wanted always to be a boy and have fun!" Peter continued. "So I ran away to Kensington Gardens, and then I met Tink."

"Tink?" said Wendy.

"Tinker Bell," Peter said proudly. "She is my fairy."

Wendy laughed. "But there are no such things—"

Quickly, Peter quickly cut her off. "No!" he cried. "Don't say that! Every time somebody says that, there is a fairy somewhere who falls down dead!"

Wendy's mouth snapped shut. She certainly didn't want to harm any fairies. "How dreadful," said Wendy.

"Tink goes with me everywhere," Peter Pan explained. "We came here to listen to the stories. I like the one about the prince who couldn't find the lady who wore glass slippers."

"Cinderella!" Wendy said. "That story ended when the prince finally found her and they lived happily ever after."

Peter Pan's smile lit up his whole face. "I knew it!" he cried.

Wendy stepped close to the wild boy just then.

"Peter," she whispered. "I should like to give you . . . a thimble."

"What's that?" said Peter, perplexed.

At that, Wendy puckered her lips, closed her eyes, and leaned close to Peter. The boy stepped back fearfully.

"You mustn't touch me," he warned.

Wendy opened her eyes again. "Why?"

"I don't know," Peter replied. "No one ever touches me."

"It won't hurt," Wendy promised.

He took one look in Wendy's eyes and Peter's heart melted. The boy stood up straight, waiting for Wendy to kiss him. She puckered her lips and leaned close . . .

Suddenly, the drawer of the sideboard burst open. Out flew Tinker Bell, who burned across the nursery room like an angry comet. And she was heading right for Wendy.

Tink seized Wendy's long hair and yanked her away from Peter. Wendy howled in pain.

"Tink, stop it!" Peter Pan cried. He pulled Tinker Bell off Wendy and hurled the little fairy across the room. Tink tumbled through the air to land with a plop on Wendy's pillow.

Wendy smoothed down her hair.

"She is not very polite," Peter warned. "Tink says if you try to give me a thimble again she will kill you."

"Oh!" said Wendy. "And I had supposed fairies to be charming."

Tinker Bell leaped off the pillow and into the air. The ball of light streaked across the room to the open window, leaving a trail of sparkling fairy dust. There Tinker Bell hovered, as if she were waiting. But what was she waiting for?

Suddenly, Wendy knew. She took the wild boy's hand. "Peter, don't go," she pleaded.

"But I must tell the others about Cinderella," Peter said. He shook Wendy's hand loose and hopped on to the window ledge.

"But . . . I know lots of stories," Wendy said.

"Why, the stories I could tell the Lost Boys!"

Peter jumped down from the window ledge again. He took Wendy's hand in his.

"Come with me!" he said.

"I . . . I cannot fly," Wendy replied, frowning.

"I'll teach you," Peter said.

Wendy's mind was reeling. A part of her wanted to go with Peter Pan and visit Neverland. But another part of her wanted to stay safe at home with her family. As she thought about Peter's offer, Wendy's eyes moved to the sleeping forms of her little brothers.

"Could John and Michael come, too?" Wendy asked.

Peter shrugged, as if to say "why not?"

"John! Michael!" Wendy cried, shaking her brothers awake. "There is a boy here who is to teach us to fly."

Michael rubbed his eyes sleepily as John fumbled for his spectacles. He put them on and stared at Peter Pan.

"You offend reason, sir," John declared when he saw Peter Pan's outlandish attire of jungle leaves, bark, and feathers – all patched together in some mysterious manner. Quite unlike proper English boys, thought John, who wore long nightshirts to bed.

Peter said nothing back to John. He simply floated off the floor. Then he spun into a graceful backwards somersault, turned slowly in the air several times, and finally landed, light as a feather, on the headboard of John's bed.

John's eyes were as big as tea cups. His mouth gaped wide in amazement. Then he hopped out of bed and ran to Peter Pan's side.

"I should like to offend it with you!" said John.

Peter smiled, then bent low and whispered the secret of flight to John, Michael and Wendy.

"You just think happy thoughts," whispered Peter. Then, rising like a balloon full of hot air, he threw his arms wide. "And they lift you into the air!"

"I've got it! I've got it!" John cried. Using his bed like a runway, John bent his head low and charged forward, to launch himself into the air.

"Swords . . . Daggers . . . Napoleon . . ." he cried.

John landed on the floor and tumbled into a corner. "Ouch!" he cried.

Peter Pan frowned. Then he grabbed Tinker Bell and shook her until the little fairy's head span. A tinkling rain of golden fairy dust settled over John, and he grinned.

Michael, meanwhile, hopped on to the bed. He was ready to fly – or so he thought.

"Pudding . . . ice-cream . . . mudpies . . . never-having-to-take-a-bath-again . . ." the little boy chanted.

Then Michael dived head-first off the bed. On the way to the floor, he flew right through a shower of fairy dust. Instead of bouncing off the hardwood floor, Michael found himself floating weightlessly.

"I'm flying! I'm flying!" he cried.

Finally, Michael came to rest on top of a high bookshelf that stood against one wall of the cluttered nursery.

"I flewed! I flewed!" Michael cried triumphantly.

Outside, in her kennel, Nana saw the children flying around the nursery. She barked madly and strained at her chain until she broke free.

In the nursery, Peter blew a puff of fairy dust from his pale hand. The dust sprinkled over Wendy and sparkling grains shimmered in her hair. With a squeal of delight, Wendy rose into the air!

"Come away!" Peter Pan cried, floating at her side. "Come away to Neverland."

"Oh," Wendy cried. "But what about Mother?"

Suddenly her anxiety sank Wendy to earth again. John and Michael both settled onto the floor by her side.

"Father . . ." said John.

"Nana . . ." said little Michael.

"There are mermaids," said Peter Pan.

"Mermaids?" said Wendy with interest, and she began to rise into the air again.

"Indians," Peter Pan whispered softly.

"Indians!" John and Michael cried together, and then they were floating, too.

"And pirates," said Peter.

"Pirates!" John, Michael and Wendy squealed with glee. Now all of them were flying circles around the nursery.

Suddenly, John soared through the window, scattering the lace curtains behind him. Michael circled the room again, snatched up his teddy bear from his pillow, then followed his brother out.

Only Wendy hesitated.

Peter took her hand. Together they drifted to the window and landed. As Wendy's bare foot touched the ledge, she turned back around and looked at the nursery door.

Wendy could not stop thinking of her mother and father, of Aunt Millicent, of everything they expected of her.

"Forget them," Peter Pan whispered to her. "Come with me where you'll never, never have to worry about grown-up things again."

"Never is an awfully long time," Wendy whispered.

Then she looked beyond the identical grey rooftops of London, to the promise of buoyant clouds and curious stars. Even the lively winter breeze seemed to whisper *Come away, come away* . . . as it pulled at her nightgown and tugged at her long brown hair.

Wendy turned her gaze back to Peter, and his blue eyes locked with hers. Then he smiled. It was a roguish smile. A smile of disobedience and daring. A smile no girl could resist.

And, so, Wendy made the decision. Clutching tightly to his hand, she stepped off the ledge . . .

Suddenly, Mr and Mrs Darling and Nana burst into the nursery. Earlier, when Nana had broken free of her chain, she'd raced down the street to the grand party where Mr and Mrs Darling had gone for the evening.

The barking dog had barrelled through the drawing room door, leaping up, urging the Darlings to follow. Knowing that something was most definitely wrong, Mr and Mrs Darling had indeed followed Nana back to the house, then up the stairs to the very nursery where they now stood.

It would have been delightful for these parents

to have found their children all tucked up in their nests. What relief there would have been had they arrived in time. What joy to have found their little birds had not flown. But what use would that have been? Then the story would have to end here. And indeed it doesn't!

5

The Island Come True

As Wendy skimmed the rooftops, the lights of the city twinkled like sapphires beneath her. The stars above gleamed white and yellow and blue. Clouds were fluffy and cool, the moon was full, bright, and never so close as now.

Together, Peter Pan, Wendy, John and Michael lifted high into the vast night sky. They rose and rose and rose, until all that could be seen from the ground were four shadows. Those shadows raced at dizzying speed towards a sea of moonlit clouds.

As the four plunged into the clouds, Peter Pan twisted his arms and turned in the air. Now they were racing towards the pole star, sparkling like a beacon in the night.

Peter turned to John. "Who are you?" he asked.

"I'm John," the boy replied nervously.

"Well, John," said Peter. "Take hold of this."

Peter offered John his ankle. John gripped it tightly.

"Pass it on," Peter Pan commanded.

John turned to his little brother.

"Take hold of my ankle," he cried through the whistling wind. Michael stretched out his arms and grabbed his older brother's leg.

"Whatever happens," Peter Pan warned them both. "DON'T . . . LET . . . GO!"

With a sonic boom, Peter burst forward, into a white-hot line of streaking speed. John, Michael and Wendy hung on for dear life. The air rushing by threatened to tear the group asunder and scatter them to the four winds.

Wendy shrieked, for she was the tail of this human comet. She spun and spun, hanging on, as the four of them plunged into the heart of the pole star!

An ear-shattering explosion buffeted their ears as the heavenly body seemed to fly apart. Suddenly they were sucked into a vast tunnel of blinding light. Peter pushed ahead, leading them through the centre of the star. Beams of light sparkled off his head and shoulders. Peter just tucked his chin into his neck and pushed on even faster.

Then, suddenly, all was quiet as they shot out of the tunnel of light, and tumbled gracefully through a galaxy of burning stars.

Michael's arms flung wide and he let go of his teddy bear. It dropped from his hand to splash into the firmament. Ripples appeared, and only then did Wendy, John and Michael realise they were floating over a vast, calm, shoreless ocean. The water shimmered darkly beneath them like the surface of a black mirror.

They flew on until they saw something in the distance rising up from the horizon to stab the sky. It was a jagged snow-capped mountain peak. Bathed in golden rays, it towered over a green island completely blanketed with thick jungles.

"Neverland," Wendy gasped with wonder as

they raced over the starry waves towards the green island ahead.

When Peter and the children reached a lush valley, they cried and pointed. There were teepees, dozens of them. A whole Mohican village! As hundreds of Indian children ran out of their tents, to frolic in a vast field of flowers, John and Michael gaped in awe.

The passing of Peter Pan and his newfound friends did not go unnoticed by other, less friendly folk.

Beneath a tangle of vines, under the canopy of a hundred vast trees, was a shadowy lagoon called Pirates Cove. There floated a ship called the *Jolly Roger*, the very ship Captain Hook and his band of cutthroats, rogues, and villains called home.

On the deck of the huge sailing ship, which was stuck in a frozen sea of ice, a band of scurvy pirates diced and drank and brawled and napped. But as the comet that was Peter Pan and his friends streaked over their heads, all eyes turned skyward to watch its passing.

Only Smee, the ship's boatswain and the man

on watch duty, missed the comet. He was sound asleep.

When the comet passed, the rickety wooden door to the Captain's cabin creaked open. Out scuttled the ugliest, scrawniest, featherless, one-eyed, peg-legged parrot in the universe. The bird cocked its waddled head, then hopped towards its favourite victim.

Plump and sweating, Smee the boatswain napped peacefully on deck. He was snoring loudly, his toes sticking out of his battered shoes. Unnoticed by the boatswain, the parrot waddled to Smee's side. Finally, the bird hopped onto a barrel sitting next to the sleeping pirate. Leaning close to Smee's ear, the parrot unleashed the loudest, most annoying *SQUAAAARRRWWK* anyone had ever heard!

Smee shrieked himself awake, then fell against the barrel. Arms flailing, he tumbled to the deck. The parrot scurried out of the way as the other pirates laughed.

Sputtering, an angry Smee jumped to his feet. From a thick leather belt that circled his ample waist, the boatswain drew a flintlock pistol. He aimed the weapon at the bird and pulled the trigger. In an explosion of noise, fire and smoke, the parrot vanished.

"Devil bird!" Smee cursed.

The peg-legged bird reappeared. This time it peeked from around a corner. And with a triumphant caw, the parrot flittered away.

Rubbing his sleepy eyes, Smee didn't notice the bird's escape, but he did notice the sound of ice cracking. He peeked over the rail. Sure enough, cracks were breaking up the ice all over the frozen cove. Smiling devilishly, Smee waddled to the captain's cabin.

"Cap'n?" Smee called, opening the door.

Inside the cabin, a single flickering light pierced the gloom. Smee could see a shape lurking in the shadows, just beyond the captain's heavy oak desk.

"Cap'n," Smee said. "As I was sittin' wide-eyed on me watch, I noticed winter-time on the water, but spring-time on the trees . . ."

No sound came from the darkness, save the sound of heavy breathing.

"I says to myself 'that's early for spring to be astir'," Smee continued nervously. "Why, spring's not due till 3pm!"

Smee approached the desk and placed his pocket watch on its surface.

"Check the time yaself, Cap'n," Smee insisted. "It—"

But before Smee could finish his thought, a sharp steel hook swung out of the darkness and smashed the watch to pieces. Smee jumped backwards. Out of the shadows, a dim shape emerged – Captain James Hook, the most notorious and evil pirate of them all!

His hair, black and shiny as boot polish, hung in ringlets from his head. His blue eyes glowed eerily. He wore a long, dark pirate cloak and a single earring gleamed in the dim light. But the most amazing thing was Hook's hand – for it wasn't a hand at all! All that was there was a rusty, curved hook.

"I was dreaming," snarled Captain Hook. "Of Pan."

"Pan, Cap'n?"

As he spoke, Smee lowered his eyes. He didn't like it when Captain Hook spoke of Peter Pan. Bad things usually happened.

"I was tearing him so splendidly," Captain Hook said, purring with satisfaction. "And in the dream I was a kindly fellow, full of forgiveness . . . I thanked Peter Pan for cutting off my hand and giving me this fine hook for gutting bellies and ripping throats, and for other such uses as combing my hair and opening jars."

Captain Hook's eyes burned fiercely, and Smee could see the scarlet in them, just like when the Captain was ripping bellies.

"So Pan done ya a favour then, Cap'n?" said Smee.

Captain Hook stepped out of the shadows and gripped Smee by his collar.

"A favour!" he bellowed, holding his dull, rusty hook in front of Smee's nose. "You call this rusting monstrosity a favour?"

Smee quaked in his battered shoes.

"Peter Pan threw my hand to a crocodile!" Hook ranted. "And the brute liked the taste so much it has followed me ever since, licking its lips at the thought of eating the rest of me!"

Hook shoved Smee aside. The boatswain stumbled against the desk.

"Thank Lucifer the brute swallowed a clock that goes *tick*, *tick*, *tick* inside of him, or the crocodile would have had me before now."

Hook scooped up the remains of the shattered pocket watch and carried the pieces to a small wooden box. The pirate captain dumped the broken pieces into the box. It was nearly filled to the brim with shattered clocks of all shapes and sizes.

"When I was a lad, I was offered a clerkship in the city," Hook said. "If I had taken it, there wouldn't be a more honest man alive today."

Captain Hook sunk into a chair and beat his head with his hand and his hook. "But to be tortured forever just because I took a wrong turn," he moaned.

Then the Captain looked up, into the eyes of the nervous boatswain.

"Why did you wake me, Smee?" Hook demanded.

While he waited for an answer, the pirate captain rose and walked to a wood-burning stove. As Smee watched, Hook plunged his metal hand into a bubbling vat of acid that cooked and smoked over the fire. There was a loud hiss and a sizzle.

"Like I said, Cap'n," Smee replied. "The ice is thawin', the sun is out, the flowers in bloom."

Hook withdrew his metal hand from the vat and held it up to the light. The hook now gleamed like it was shiny and new. But the captain's eyes continued to burn a flickering red.

"He's back," Hook growled menacingly, "Peter Pan has returned to Neverland."

6

The Lost Boys

Peter, Wendy, John and Michael had hidden themselves in the white, fleecy clouds above the gloomy
Pirates' Cove. Peter Pan watched the deck of the
Jolly Roger through a long spyglass. After a while,
he handed the telescope to Wendy.

"Forty gunner," Wendy said, after studying
the ship. "She must do fourteen knots under full
sail."

John took the spyglass and peered through it.
Suddenly he gasped.

"Hook!" he cried.

Peter Pan snatched the spyglass from John's

grip. He watched as Captain Hook strutted across the wooden deck.

"Is Hook very big?" Michael asked nervously.

Peter looked through the spyglass again. Then he gazed at the ship without the spyglass.

"Not as big as he was!" Peter chuckled. "Let's take a closer look."

Peter waved his arms, and their hiding-place cloud moved closer to the cove. Suddenly, a gust of wind blew John's Napoleon hat from his head. He tried to snatch it back, but it quickly drifted out of his reach.

Peter Pan and his friends weren't the only ones to have a spyglass. At that moment, Captain Hook raised his own. Squinting, he peered through it, scanning the shoreline and the jungle beyond.

Just then, John's Napoleon hat floated out of the sky and landed on the ugly parrot's bald head. The bird cawed indignantly.

Hook tilted his spyglass up, to stare intently at a large cloud and the blue sky around it. Then the pirate captain saw them – four figures silhouetted by the sunlight streaming down behind the cloud they had hidden in. Captain Hook's lips curled into a sneering smile.

"Fetch Long Tom," Hook commanded. And his pirate crew quickly sprang to prepare their secret weapon.

"There is some sort of activity on deck," said Peter, still gazing through his spyglass.

He watched as the pirates rolled a long-barrelled cannon into view and loaded it. Then, to Peter's surprise, the pirates pointed the cannon at their cloud!

Before Peter could cry out a warning, Smee touched a torch to the fuse. The cannon fired in a blast of smoke. The cannonball ripped through the cloud, scattering it. And the whoosh of its swift journey swept Wendy from her perch. With a gasp, she tumbled off the cloud.

Shrieking, her brothers fell through the hole made by the cannonball. At the very last second, John caught a wisp of vapour and hung on. Michael caught John's ankle and hung on, too. Screaming, and kicking their legs, the boys dangled high over the green jungle below.

On the deck of the pirate ship, the crew reloaded the cannon called Long Tom. Then they pointed it at the boys.

Peter ignored John's cries for help and Michael's screams.

"Tink!" Peter cried. "Find Wendy! Leave the rest to me."

Trailing white-hot light like a shooting star, Tinker Bell took off after the fallen girl. Peter Pan looked down at the pirate ship, then dived off the cloud. The pirates gasped as Peter Pan swooped out of the sky towards the ship.

"Pan!" Hook cried, pushing Long Tom's barrel. "Keep up with him. Keep him in your sights!"

Smee turned the cannon on Peter Pan.

"I've got you now," Hook said, shaking his fist. "Fire!"

KA-BOOM!

To Hook's surprise, the cannonball blasted right through the main mast. With a loud crack, the wood split and the mast and sail plunged onto the deck of the *Jolly Roger*.

John and Michael, still hanging from the cloud, trod air.

"Michael," shouted John. "Are you shot?"

"I haven't checked yet," Michael yelled back. "But there's something worse."

"What could be worse?" said John.

"My thoughts," Michael replied. "They . . . aren't . . . very . . . happy!"

With a sound like ripping fabric, the cloud fell apart. With a final scream, John and Michael plunged to earth.

"Swords," John cried, flapping his arms like crazy. "Daggers . . . Napoleon . . ."

But nothing could stop their plunge through the tops of the trees. A moment later, John and Michael landed with a splash in the chilly, foam-flecked waters of a wild, roaring river!

Wendy, meanwhile, had kept good thoughts in her head. She could still fly, but unfortunately she was lost in the clouds.

She wandered for a few minutes, calling for Peter, for John, even for Michael. No one replied.

Suddenly, Wendy saw a cloud that seemed to glow with a magical light.

"Tinker Bell?" she called.

Tink burst from the cloud and flew away, annoyed that she had been found by the hated Wendy.

Now Tinker Bell may seem altogether bad, just now. But she was not always this way. Sometimes she was altogether good. Fairies are so small that there is no room in them to be partly bad and partly good. They must be completely one thing or the other at any moment in time. And at this moment, Tinker Bell was completely jealous of Wendy.

"Tink?" Wendy called more loudly. "Tink! I don't know where I'm going."

A fact that didn't bother Tinker Bell in the least!

Back on the deck of the Jolly Roger, chaos had broken out.

"Re-load the cannon!" Captain Hook bellowed.

"But Pan's gone," said Skylights, one of Hook's pirate henchmen.

Hook pulled out his pistol and fired on Skylights. The shot pirate pitched overboard, head first. Poor Skylights just wasn't evil enough for Hook!

"Search the jungle," Hook cried. "Bring me those children!"

Wendy flew though the clouds, trying to keep up with Tinker Bell. But the fairy wouldn't slow down, and soon Wendy lost sight of her.

Meanwhile, down in the valley below, curious eyes were watching Wendy approach. The Lost Boys were on the prowl, and nothing got past them! Like Peter, the boys were clad in leaves, feathers, bark and leather. They had bows and arrows slung over their shoulders and one of them, named Slightly, gazed at the sky through a spyglass.

Slightly was a boy who liked to cut whistles out of the trees and dance wildly to his own tunes. He was also the most arrogant of the boys because he believed he still remembered the days before he was lost and this gave his nose an annoying tilt.

"It is a large white bird," Slightly declared with his ever-present confidence. He lowered the glass and his nose crinkled up in disgust. "Quite ugly, too."

Suddenly a ball of light darted over their heads.

"Hello, Tink," said Tootles. "Where's Peter?"

Poor Tootles was a brave boy, but he never had the chance to prove it. You see, big things happened all the time in Neverland, but they always seemed to happen when Tootles was gone. The day would be quiet, and Tootles would wander off to pick berries. Then he'd return to find the others had just fought some fantastic battle.

This bad luck would have made some boys angry. But not Tootles. Instead of making him angry, this bad luck had made Tootles a little bit sad and the most understanding and kind of all the Lost Boys. It had also made him the most trusting, and, therefore, the most easily tricked.

Poor sweet Tootles. When Tinker Bell floated

down and whispered in his ear, she had already decided to take advantage of his trusting nature.

Tootles listened carefully to Tink, nodding once or twice. Then Tinker Bell flitted away and Tootles turned to his fellow Lost Boys.

"Tink says the bird is called a 'Wendy' and Peter wants us to shoot it," he explained, drawing his bow.

"We have our orders," Slightly declared, again with confidence. "Shoot the Wendybird!"

Tootles, thrilled to be finally proving himself to Peter Pan, aimed his arrow and let it fly. The arrow flew straight and true. And, to the amazement of the Lost Boys, who secretly doubted Tootles' skill, the arrow struck the Wendybird. The pale creature crumpled, then dropped from the sky.

"I got it! I got it!" cried Tootles.

The Lost Boys immediately searched for their prey, crashing through the forest until they arrived at a small clearing. In the tall grass, the Wendybird lay motionless, an arrow in her chest.

"That is no bird," said Nibs, perplexed.

"It is a *lady*," Curly proclaimed.

"And Tootles has killed her," said Slightly. (Still

confident, of course – but this time in blaming Tootles!)

Nibs gasped. "Now I see," he cried. "Peter was bringing her to us! A *lady* to take care of us."

"And Tootles . . ." said Curly with a sob.

"Tootles has killed her!" all the boys cried. All of them but poor, kind, sweet, gentle Tootles.

"I did it," Tootles said, a tear touching his pink cheek. "When a lady came to me in dreams I said 'Pretty Mother!' But when she really came I shot her!"

Suddenly, Peter Pan dropped out of the sky behind the Lost Boys.

"Hullo, boys," he said cheerfully. "I am back."

When the boys saw Peter Pan, they grouped together to hide poor Wendy's body.

"Great news!" said Peter with a grin. "I know what happened to Cinderella. She defeated the pirates, married the Prince, and lived happily ever after!"

The boys nodded in approval. But their reaction was not the one Peter expected. Something was up . . .

"Greater news," said Peter. "I have brought you she that told of Cinderella! She is to tell us stories! She is . . ."

Just then the boys parted, to finally reveal Wendy.

". . . dead."

From her perch on a nearby branch, Tinker Bell laughed, a tinkling sound like a wind chime on a chilly wind.

Peter knelt over Wendy, and plucked the arrow from her chest.

"Whose arrow?" he asked without looking at them.

The Lost Boys shifted and lowered their eyes to the ground. Finally, poor Tootles spoke.

"Mine, Peter."

Peter held the arrow in his hand. He twirled it, then caught it again, arrowhead down. Then he raised up his arm, pointing the sharp tip at Tootles.

Instantly, the boy fell to his knees before Peter Pan and bared his chest.

"Strike, Peter!" Tootles cried. "Strike true."

They were interrupted by a moan of pain.

"The Wendy lives!" cried Curly.

Once again, Peter fell to his knees before Wendy. His hand moved to where the arrow had struck. Parting her nightgown, Peter saw that the sharp arrowhead had struck – but not her heart. It had been stopped by the acorn necklace he'd given her.

"My kiss!" Peter cried, amazed. "My kiss saved her."

Slightly, the boy who liked to say he remembered the time before he was lost, became very excited. "I remember kisses!" he cried. "Let me see it."

Peter showed him the acorn, pierced deeply by the arrow.

"Aye, that is a kiss," said Slightly with confidence. "A powerful thing."

Nibs looked down at Wendy. She was moving, but was not yet fully awake. "We cannot leave her out or she will spoil," he said.

"Let us carry her down to the house," suggested Slightly.

"Wait," said Curly. "Is it sufficiently respectful for us to touch the Wendy?"

Peter regarded the Lost Boys' dirty hands and shook his head. "No, it is not."

Tootles scratched his head. "What shall we do?"

Slightly shrugged. "She must stay here and die."

"No!" said Peter, shaking his head. "We will build a house around her."

The Lost Boys cheered Peter's brilliant idea. Then they immediately set to work. Curly cut branches. Tootles pruned leaves. Two boys called The Twins (who stuck together like twins and who Peter could never tell apart) strung vines. Slightly pounded logs into the ground around the sleeping girl.

After a time, one of The Twins (he couldn't tell which) whispered in Peter Pan's ear. Peter nodded and walked into the forest, where he found Tinker Bell. The fairy was sulking on a branch.

"Was it you, Tink?" Peter asked. "You that told the Lost Boys to hurt Wendy?"

The tinkling sound that Tinker Bell made was her answer. The stubborn fairy was proud of what she did.

"Then I am your friend no more," Peter Pan

declared, his eyes flashing with anger. "Begone from me for ever!"

Peter turned his back on Tink and stormed off.

The little fairy curled into a tiny ball of misery. Her fairy light dimmed, and Tinker Bell flew away, so none of the Lost Boys could see her cry.

7

The Little House

Wendy awoke to the sound of hammering. How strange, she thought. The last thing she remembered was flying through the clouds. Had it all been a dream? Would Nana lick her face when she opened her eyes? Would John and Michael demand a story?

Then the hammering sounded again, and slowly Wendy lifted her eyelids. She found herself in a primitive hut made of wood – and poorly made at that. Wendy squinted against the beams of bright, afternoon sunlight which poured through gaps in the walls. There were holes in the roof, too.

Indeed, Wendy doubted this building would hold back an English rainstorm.

As Wendy sat up, she saw a rough-hewn wooden door. She went to it and threw it open.

Outside, the Lost Boys were hard at work. Some carried wood from the forest. Others laid leaves and branches on the roof to keep out the weather. But when the boys saw Wendy, they all stopped working and bowed. Those that wore hats – of cloth or fur or feathered Indian headdresses – were polite enough to remove them in the presence of a lady.

"Wendy-lady," said Slightly, bowing deeper than anyone else – for he still remembered the customs and manners of the world before he'd become lost. "It is for you that we built this house, with a door-knocker and a chimney."

Wendy glanced at the door. It did indeed have a large, brass door-knocker. And there was a chimney, too, though it was crooked and looked like a stiff wind would blow it over. But she was touched by their efforts, and turned to thank them.

That's when all the Lost Boys, every last one, fell on their knees before her.

"Please be our mother!" they cried.

"Oh!" said Wendy, startled.

"Please," said Tootles, reaching out his arms. "Be my pretty mother!"

"Well," said Wendy. "It is frightfully fascinating, but . . . Well, you see, I have no real experience."

"Do you tell stories?" asked Nibs.

"Yes," said Wendy, who was proud of her story-telling skills.

"Then you are perfect," cried Curly.

Wendy thought about it for a moment. Then she nodded her head. "Very well," she said. "I will do my best."

At that, the boys jumped to their feet and cheered. Then they surrounded Wendy and led her to a large, twisted old tree near the edge of the clearing.

"Come and meet Father," Nibs said.

As she approached the old tree, Wendy spied an opening in the bark. There was darkness beyond the threshold. Before she could back away, the Lost Boys pushed her through the opening.

Wendy found herself falling and she squealed.

She slid down a smooth, sloped tunnel filled with tangled tree roots and stabbing beams of sunlight. Before she could stop herself, Wendy landed with a soft plop on a carpet of spongy moss.

She blinked and looked around. She was sitting in a huge underground cave. The flickering light of a roaring fire was the only light. There were twisted tree roots all around. Shrubs, flowers and a few saplings grew out of the floor. At last, Wendy saw a shape on the opposite side of the cavern – a figure perched regally on a huge wooden throne.

Wendy stepped around the fire to meet the leader of Neverland. She gasped when she saw Peter Pan sitting on the throne, a crown atop the golden curls on his head.

"Welcome, Mother, to our happy home under the ground," said Peter, rising.

The Lost Boys began to emerge from a dozen other entrances. Soon they crowded the chamber.

"Discipline!" Peter Pan cried. "That's what fathers believe in."

Peter focused a stern eye on the Lost Boys. "The

children tried to kill you," Peter declared. "They must die."

Peter pulled out a long cutlass and waved it in the air. Then he began to chase the terrified Lost Boys around the cave.

"Mother!" they cried. "Save us from Father."

Wendy stepped in front of Peter and took his arm. Carefully, she lowered the sword.

"Father," she said in that firmly persuasive way of mothers. "I agree they are perfectly horrid. But kill them and they shall think themselves important."

Peter rubbed his chin, listening.

"I suggest something more dreadful," Wendy continued. "Medicine!"

The Lost Boys groaned.

Wendy plucked one of the tulips that was growing out of the floor. Then she bent a leaf from a sapling, until rainwater trickled into the bud.

"This medicine is the most beastly stuff," Wendy declared. "The sticky, sweet kind."

Again the boys groaned. For in Neverland, pretending a thing would make it so. And Wendy's pretend-medicine was sure to taste as beastly as the real kind.

Wendy handed the flower to Slightly. The boy took it, but his courage quickly fled. He thrust the tulip at Peter Pan.

"Father must take it first!" Slightly insisted.

"What a splendid idea, Slightly," said Wendy. "Father should take it first, as an example to us all!"

The Lost Boys jumped up and down, cheering Wendy's plan. Wendy gave Peter the tulip. He took it nervously.

"I am not afraid of pirates," said Peter Pan. "I am not afraid of Indians. Why would I be afraid of this?"

Peter closed his eyes and put the tulip to his lips. In one big gulp, he swallowed it down.

"There!" he said, his voice stricken.

Peter looked pale and sick, but he managed to remain calm.

"Now I go to stand guard," he said, rubbing his tummy. "Because fathers stand guard . . . don't they?"

"Oh, yes," Wendy replied. "My own father . . ."

But Wendy's voice trailed off. As she refilled the tulip with medicine for the Lost Boys, she searched her memory.

"What *did* my father do?" she wondered aloud. "He would say 'a little less noise in there, John,' and sometimes, 'John . . .'"

Suddenly, Wendy blinked. "John!" she cried. "And Michael! Where are my brothers?"

"Who?" said Peter Pan. He had already forgotten them.

At that moment, John and Michael were lost in a deep, dark, savage forest. They were dirty, wet, miserable and tired. And they were talking about philosophy – which is a grown-up way of trying to make sense of nonsense.

Because he was the oldest, John felt it was his duty to philosophise for Michael. He wasn't having much luck.

"The world is probable," John stated with great seriousness to Michael. "And because the world is probable, it is likely you will be sent to school, grow up, get married and die. It is *unlikely* you will fight pirates, meet fairies, or fly about. Therefore Neverland is improbable. Therefore I conclude none of this is really happening."

Michael, who was younger and therefore more apt to believe what he saw, heard and felt, rather than what he was told to believe, didn't agree. He was about to say so when a terrible roar echoed through the jungle.

The noise shook the treetops and frightened thousands of birds out of their branches. Another roar quickly followed. This one sounded even closer.

Improbable or not, John and Michael did the only thing they could think of—

They ran!

Crashing through the jungle, vines tearing at their legs, the brothers ran as fast as they could. Ahead of them, they saw rocks, then the mouth of a dark cave. They dived into the cave and huddled against the rocky wall. Beyond them the cave plunged deep into the earth.

"Hello?" whispered Michael into the darkness. His voice echoed back to him.

At the sound of his voice, millions of tiny glow worms that clung to the roof of the cave lit up. Soon their light revealed a long tunnel. Cautiously, the boys followed it.

After a long walk, the boys came to a large cavern lighted by the same magical glow worms. On the wall of the cave was a framed painting of Captain James Hook. In the picture, Hook was a young man with two good hands.

Around the painting was scattered a pirates' treasure. Silver candlesticks, sparkling jewels, delicate necklaces, golden bracelets, silverware and hundreds of gold and silver coins were scattered everywhere.

Michael and John explored the treasure room for a few moments. Then they heard the sound of a ticking clock. The boys turned to see a gigantic crocodile emerge from a side tunnel. The creature had beady yellow eyes, massive, toothy jaws, leathery flesh, and a long, thick tail that thrashed back and forth.

The crocodile moved on stubby, powerful legs, its feet tipped with sharp black claws. The beast grunted with every step, but the loudest noise of all was the sound of the clock ticking in its belly.

Hiding behind a chest full of gleaming treasure, John and Michael watched as the crocodile crawled across the cave. It paused at the painting of Captain Hook. The beast sniffed the painting, then roared with longing. It wanted to eat the Captain, not just his hand!

As they watched, the crocodile lumbered to the opposite side of the cave and curled up. Soon it closed its yellow eyes and began to snore.

The boys peeked over the edge of the treasure chest, at the sleeping beast. They were too afraid to move. Too afraid to make a sound.

Then Michael gasped. John turned and saw an amazing thing. The painting of Captain Hook had sprouted legs and was creeping out of the cave!

Before the painting got very far, the crocodile's eyes opened and the creature charged. John and Michael were so frightened that they jumped out of hiding and tried to escape.

The crocodile was faster. Quick as a wink, the creature had the brothers trapped. But before the hungry reptile could swallow them up, John grabbed the walking painting and thrust it into the crocodile's wide open jaws.

The animal clamped down its jaws, but could not close its mouth. The heavy wooden frame on the picture had wedged its jaws open.

Seeing their chance to escape, John and Michael ran, the crocodile on their heels. As quick as rabbits the boys raced up the shaft and back out into the jungle.

Soon they were crashing through the forest, their arms flapping like mad, as once again the boys desperately tried to fly.

8

Carried Off

"Swords! Daggers! Napoleon!" John cried, flapping his wings. At his side, Michael ran, too. His eyes were closed and he flapped his wings. Both boys were hoping to take off and leave the hungry crocodile behind.

Suddenly they did – but this time feet first!

Their legs flew right towards the treetops as vines tightened like nooses around their ankles. Instantly, they realised they hadn't taken flight at all. They'd stepped into a trap!

Now they hung from a branch, their nightshirts dangling around their ears.

"How humiliating," moaned John. "But at least we lost that crocodile."

Michael peeked out from beneath his nightshirt and gasped.

"John!" he cried. "There is something worser."

"What could it be?" John asked.

Suddenly John paled as he confronted the greatest horror known to an eleven-year-old boy. An eleven-year-old girl!

The girl sat on a branch, smiling down at them. She wore a dress made of soft leather, and feathers in her sable black hair. Her skin was bronze, her teeth white. She was a full-blooded North American Indian of the Mohican tribe!

The girl laughed at the upside-down English boys. John got angry and began to struggle, which only made her laugh more. Soon the girl was laughing so hard she lost her balance and fell out of the tree, landing smack at the feet of Captain Hook!

The girl screamed. Captain Hook sneered. And his cut-throat crew howled with glee.

"Princess Tiger Lily," Captain Hook said with a

lethal smile. "You give lie to the redskin's reputation for camouflage."

Two pirates reached out and grabbed Princess Tiger Lily. She struggled helplessly. Then Captain Hook loomed over her. Frightened, the girl cowered.

"We search for Peter Pan," said Captain Hook. Smee, his boatswain, translated Hook's words into the Mohican tongue.

"One could search for Peter Pan until doom cracks," Hook continued. "However, the two boys of his acquaintance were observed falling into this part of the jungle . . ."

Hook leered at the girl, his eyes gleaming. "Have you seen them?" Hook demanded.

Hanging over Hook and his pirate crew's heads, John and Michael held their breath. Princess Tiger Lily launched into a long angry-sounding speech in her native tongue. At the end of her tirade, the Princess spat at Hook's feet.

Smee listened to the girl, then turned to the captain. "She respectfully says 'no', Cap'n."

The pirate captain raised his hook and shook it in Princess Tiger Lily's pretty face.

"My hook thinks you did," said Hook. "I wonder if it would not be advisable to humour the hook?"

Captain Hook pressed his claw against Princess Tiger Lily's tender throat.

It made John furious. "I say!" he called from the tree. "Unhand that savage, you savage!"

Hook looked up to find the English brothers dangling helplessly. Quicky, Hook found the knotted vine that held them. With a single swipe of his razor-sharp claw, Hook sliced the vine and the boys came tumbling down. With gleeful cackles, the pirates hog-tied the two and dragged them away.

"Hook has your brothers," Peter Pan told Wendy.

Peter had just heard the news from the beautiful mermaids swimming in Pirates Cove, and they told Peter everything.

"John and Michael are being taken to the Black Castle," said Peter. "It is there we must go."

Wendy watched the silvery tails of the mermaids as they swam away. She'd always adored the magical creatures.

*Wendy often imagined herself aboard a pirate ship,
sword to sword with the evil James Hook.*

*Without a sound, the window slowly opened.
Peter Pan and Tinker Bell quietly sailed into the room.*

Captain Hook was quite a sight indeed.

Hook was disappointed. He didn't see the children falling from the sky.
He decided to take another shot.

The boys parted to reveal Wendy's body.
Peter fell to his knees beside her.

Suddenly a giant crocodile appeared! Its mouth was filled with razor-sharp teeth - the best kind for eating young boys.

Silently, a slender hand rose from the water and gently took hold of Wendy's wrist. The mermaid began to pull her slowly into the water.

Wendy bravely rose to her feet and revealed her sword.

Inside a hollow tree were hundreds of glowing fairies,
dancing and spinning to a lively tune.

When Wendy awoke, she found herself on the pirate ship.

Hook raised his sword and looked directly into Peter's eyes.

For many years, Wendy would tell the story of her great adventure in Neverland... second to the right and straight on till morning.

"Are mermaids not sweet?" said Wendy dreamily.

Peter's eyebrows rose. "They will sweetly drown you if you get too close. But they *do* know about pirates."

Together, Peter and Wendy went to the Black Castle. They climbed the walls and walked along the deserted parapets.

"I brought these," said Peter. He drew two swords with narrow pointed blades out of a sack and presented Wendy with one. "Can you use it?"

Wendy held her breath. She had enjoyed many a sword fight with John – but that had been with a harmless blunted toy. Could she duel as well with a real rapier?

"It's easy," said Peter. "There are three principal actions. The thrust—"

He thrust the blade at her, but Wendy jumped backwards in an effective dodge.

"The parry and the slice!" said Peter.

This time, Wendy answered his attack by swatting Peter's blade aside. Metal struck metal again, and their blades locked. Wendy and Peter came face to face. Then Peter stepped back and shook his head.

"And you a lady," he said with a smile.

Suddenly, Peter's face turned grim. "Promise me one thing. You must leave Hook to me."

Wendy nodded. "I promise."

"Then wait here for my signal," he said and turned to go.

"Wait here?" she said. "Peter . . ."

But he had already flown off to find his way into the castle.

John and Michael had been dumped into a leaky wooden longboat. The pirates had rowed and rowed and rowed. Finally, the boat had glided through a giant rusting metal gate and into the watery bowels of a crumbling dark castle.

Peeking over the edge of the boat, John and Michael saw a large rock. On top of that rock was a bleached skeleton of a long-dead pirate. It was chained to the rock with heavy, iron shackles.

Captain Hook jumped from the longboat and went to the rock. Hands on hips, he turned to face his pirate crew.

"Like all surprise attacks," barked Hook, "this one must be conducted improperly."

Hook pointed to the hog-tied brothers. "Put them on the rock!" he commanded.

Smee and Starkey clapped the boy's wrists in irons.

"Any last words?" said Smee.

"Beg for your lives," suggested Starkey.

"Sir," John said indignantly. "My brother and I are English gentlemen. English gentlemen do not beg."

"Please don't kill me!" Michael whined. "Let me live! I'll be your servant forever . . ."

That's when John began to cry for help. The pirates simply laughed, letting both boys scream their heads off as they bound them to the rock.

Wendy heard her brothers' screams and searched for a way into the castle. She came upon a tower window with bars so thick and rusted, one pull loosened the crumbling bolts.

Suddenly, she heard heavy footsteps approach. Someone had heard her movements! Wendy quickly hid behind the turret wall, peeking up to spy a dark vision from her own nightmares.

Captain Hook!

He appeared just as she'd imagined him, with pirate finery and soot black ringlets. But the eyes were what truly mesmerised her. Like prey gazing upon a predator, Wendy looked upon Hook's black bright gaze with a mixture of awe and dread.

As Hook loomed closer, Wendy took a deep breath and lifted her rapier.

But something distracted the pirate captain, and, to Wendy's relief, he suddenly turned away.

Meanwhile, Smee and Starkey had finished chaining the boys to the rock. And gagging them, too, for they grew tired of their screams. They were about to leave when heard their captain cry out to them.

"Mr Smee!" called Hook.

"Is that you, Cap'n?" said Smee.

"Odds, bobs, hammer and tongs, what do you think you're doing?" barked Hook.

"We put the children on the rock, Cap'n," said Smee, confused.

"Set them free!" commanded Hook.

"But what about your trap, Cap'n?" Smee asked.

"Set them free or I'll plunge my hook in you!"

"You heard him!" Smee cried to Starkey. "Unlock those irons."

The pirates hastily unlocked the chains and pushed the boys into the water. There, Princess Tiger Lily was waiting for them. She quickly swam away, leading John and Michael to a place in the water where they could hide.

From his hiding place in the arms of a giant stone dragon, Peter Pan cackled quietly with glee. He knew his imitation of Hook's voice would come in handy some day!

Suddenly, the two pirates heard Hook's voice boom again.

"Any sign of him?" Hook demanded.

"No, Cap'n," said Smee, really confused now.

Just then, Hook stepped out of the shadows. The *real* Hook. "Where are the children?" he demanded.

"It's all right, Cap'n," Smee said proudly. "We let 'em go."

"You what!" Hook cried.

"Y-you . . . c-called us from the s-shadows," Smee stammered. "T-told us to let 'em go."

Just then a voice that sounded very much like Hook spoke again. "Mr Smee!" it said.

Smee squealed in terror, but Hook silenced him with a wave.

"Who are you, stranger?" Hook asked.

"I am James Hook, Captain of the *Jolly Roger*," the voice replied.

"If you are Hook, then who am I?" the pirate captain demanded.

"A codfish."

"Tell me, Hook," said Captain Hook. "Do you have another name . . . Vegetable? Mineral? Animal? Man? Or boy?"

"Boy!" said the voice like Hook's.

"Ordinary boy, or wonderful boy?" Hook asked. As he spoke, the pirate followed the sound of Peter's voice, until he arrived at the dragon statue.

"Yes, wonderful" said Peter in Hook's voice. "Do you give up?"

"Yes," said Hook, climbing the statue.

Peter rose and smiled triumphantly. "I am . . ."

"Peter!" Wendy cried from her hiding place. "Look out!"

Peter turned to see Hook standing right behind him, claw raised, pistol aimed.

"We have him!" Captain Hook cried, firing his weapon.

But Peter was already gone! He'd floated up into the air, then swooped down again to grab Wendy.

They raced together towards the heavy iron gate, but it was already lowering fast. And when it slammed into the water, everyone was trapped inside the bowels of the Black Castle. Wendy and Peter Pan on the parapets. And John, Michael, and Princess Tiger Lily still hiding in the water.

Suddenly, a skiff packed with pirates, and with the cannon called Long Tom on its deck, floated out of the shadows.

Peter and Wendy turned to run in the opposite direction. But they were stopped when another skiff rounded a bend in the water and aimed another cannon at them.

Peter Pan smiled, raised his sword, and took off in flight. He swooped down on Captain Hook and their blades met with a clang.

"Only two cannons, Captain?" Peter Pan taunted.

But the pirate captain just laughed and shook his metal claw at Peter Pan.

"The game is up, boy," Hook snarled.

Some of the greatest heroes have confessed that just before they begin combat they feel a sinking in their stomachs. But Peter Pan had no such sinking feeling. With a grin, Peter nodded to the evil pirate's metal hand and asked a simple question –

"Ready to lose another one?"

9

Duel in the Castle

As Captain Hook and Peter Pan duelled with swords on the stone parapets, Wendy was confronted by a pirate named Cookson.

"Yer gonna watch or fight, girlie?" the pirate said with a sneer.

"Who be you to call me 'girlie'?" Wendy demanded, crashing her rapier against the pirate's blade. The fight was on!

Wendy slashed, cutting Cookson's cheek. "I *am* sorry!" she cried.

In reply, Cookson drew his pistol and shot the blade off Wendy's rapier! She hurled the grip at the pirate. It bounced off his fat head and sent him reeling off the ledge and into the water.

Also down in the water, Tiger Lily led Michael and John to the winch that raised the Black Castle's gate. They tried and tried to open the metal barrier, but it was too heavy – even for all three of them. Giving up, the brothers turned to see a giant pirate slash his sword at them!

John looked up in time to see Wendy on the ledge above him. She picked up Cookson's sword and tossed it to her brother. John grabbed the blade and slammed it against the giant pirate's blade. Angry, the pirate knocked John's spectacles from his face, blinding him!

The giant pirate swung his sword again. This time it cut off the head of poor Michael's teddy bear. Michael screamed with rage and charged the giant, burying his head deep into the giant pirate's unprotected stomach. With Tiger Lily's and John's help, the giant pirate ended up in the water, too!

Tiger Lily planted a victory kiss on John's cheek, and he blushed crimson.

Suddenly, loud booms sounded as both cannons

fired at Peter Pan. But instead of cannonballs, the guns fired rope netting to entangle Peter and bring him down!

Wendy looked on in horror as Peter struggled to free himself. Hook laughed in mocking triumph from his perch on the dragon statue. He signalled Cecco, who aimed Long Tom's muzzle at the tangled Peter.

"I have waited long for this moment!" Hook cried.

Cecco bent and touched his torch to Long Tom's fuse. It caught fire, just as Wendy seized a vine and swung over the water.

With a single kick, Wendy knocked Cecco and his burning torch off the barge. But it was too late, for Long Tom was firing!

Unfortunately for Hook, Cecco had bumped the cannon as he fell. Now the muzzle was aimed at the huge dragon statue!

With a huge explosion, the base of the statue shattered and it tumbled over – sending Captain Hook and Peter Pan into the water with a giant splash.

Hook swam to the rock. So did Peter. They climbed to the tip of the ledge and faced one another once more. From her place on the floating barge, Wendy watched the struggle.

"And now, Peter Pan, you shall die!" roared Hook.

Peter's grin simply grew wider. "To die will be an awfully big adventure."

Suddenly, a dark shadow loomed over Captain Hook. The sound of ticking made Hook turn pale. He turned to see the hungry crocodile snapping its jaws and charging!

Peter instantly took flight. But Hook managed to grab his ankle and both of them soared away from the rock.

The pirate was heavy and weighed Peter down as he climbed up Peter's leg and got a grip on his sword belt. But Peter thought fast and unsnapped his belt, letting Hook plunge into the water. The crocodile dived off the rock, swimming towards its prey.

Smee rowed hard to help his commander.

Peter flew to Wendy's barge and landed at her

side. Then they rescued John, Michael and Tiger Lily from the water. Finally, they made for the gate, which John had managed to wedge open with his sword.

As the children rowed through the iron gate, Peter snatched the bow and arrows from Tiger Lily's back.

"May I?" he asked. Tiger Lily nodded.

Peter turned and aimed the bow at Hook. At the very last minute, he shifted the weapon. When he fired, the arrow struck the sword that wedged the gate open. It crashed down again, trapping Hook, Smee and the hungry crocodile in the watery underground grotto.

It would be delightful to report that the crocodile ate Captain Hook.

But then, the book would have to end here. And indeed it doesn't!

That night in the Mohican village, a gigantic bonfire reached into the starry sky. Its flickering light illuminated the happy faces of the Indians as they danced in celebration of the victory over Hook.

Dancing with them were John, Michael and all the Lost Boys.

Not present were Peter and Wendy.

Deep in the forest, Peter was leading Wendy to a very special place. As they moved quietly through the trees, Wendy spied the magical light of the fairies. The mysterious creatures were flitting up and down and all around them!

Soon Peter and Wendy arrived at an enormous tree with a cave at its roots. Hundreds of fairies streamed into that cave. Inside, all the fairies of Neverland danced in a fairy ballroom. Wendy peered into the cave to watch, her eyes wide with wonder.

"What do you think, old lady?" Peter asked.

"Old lady?" said Wendy, indignant.

Peter scratched his head. "Michael told me mothers are called 'old lady,'" he said.

Wendy smiled. "I think I should like to dance," she announced.

"Dance away," said Peter, with a wave of his hand.

"With you," Wendy replied. She took Peter's

hand. "It will be a different kind of adventure, Peter," she told him.

As they danced, boy and girl rose into the air. The dark forest, the fairies – everything seemed to fade for them. On a nearby branch, Tinker Bell watched Peter and Wendy dance and her fairy light dimmed even more.

But Captain Hook was also in the forest that night. Though he wore a bandage around his head and his eyes were bloodshot from lack of sleep, Hook would not give up his hunt for the elusive Peter Pan!

Following the sound of the fairy music, Hook spied Peter and Wendy dancing.

"Pan dancing with a Wendy?" Hook snarled. "Oh, evil day! He has found himself a Wendy while Hook is all alone."

Leaning against a tree, Hook heard a sound like the ringing of a sad wind chime. He looked up to see Tinker Bell sitting dejectedly on a branch.

"You, too?" said Hook. Tinker Bell tinkled sadly.

"He banished you?" said Hook sympathetically. "The dog!"

Tinker Bell flitted down to Hook and began to sob on his cuff. "There, there," cooed the pirate. "Perhaps you and I should talk."

Back at the fairy tree, the music ended. But Wendy refused to let go of Peter. Together they floated over the dark treetops.

Peter studied Wendy. Her serious gaze was making him a little nervous. "Wendy," he whispered. "It is only make-believe, isn't it? That you and I are . . ."

"Oh, yes," Wendy replied.

Peter's sigh of relief made Wendy sad all of a sudden, and they floated to the ground again.

"You see," said Peter apologetically. "It would make me seem so old to be a *real* father."

"Peter," Wendy said softly. "What are your real feelings for me?"

Peter was puzzled by the word. "Feelings?"

"What you feel," Wendy continued. "Happiness. Sadness. Jealousy."

"Jealousy!" Peter cried. "Tink!"

"And anger?" said Wendy.

"Hook!" Peter swiftly replied.

"Love?" Wendy said with a sigh.

"Love?" said Peter. "I have never heard of it."

"I think you have, Peter," Wendy replied. "I daresay you have felt it yourself, for something or . . ."

Wendy paused, which made Peter very nervous indeed!

"Never!" cried Peter. "Even the sound of it offends me."

Wendy took Peter's hand, but he yanked it away. "Why do you want to spoil everything?" he protested. "We have fun, don't we? I taught you to fight and to fly! What more could there be?"

"There is so much more," Wendy exclaimed.

"What?"

Wendy thought about it for a moment before she replied. "I don't know," she confessed. "I think it becomes clearer when you grow up."

"Grow up?" growled Peter. "I will not grow up! You cannot make me! I will banish you like Tinker Bell."

Wendy put her hands on her hips and threw her head back. "I will not be banished!"

"Then go home!" Peter cried. "Go home and grow up, and take your *feelings* with you!"

Without another word, Peter soared into the air and vanished.

"Peter!" Wendy called. "Peter, come back . . ."

But Peter rocketed high into the sky, and never looked back, not even once.

10

The Pirate Ship

After Peter Pan was gone, Wendy stumbled through the dark forest until she came to the little house the Lost Boys had built for her. She went inside, curled up on the wooden floor and began to sob. Wendy cried and cried so much that she cried herself to sleep.

Then, when the moon sunk behind the trees and the night was at its darkest, the pirates of the *Jolly Roger* crept out of the forest. Silently, they surrounded Wendy's little house. Without a sound, they gently lifted it, floor and all!

When the pirates heaved the building onto their

strong shoulders, Tinker Bell appeared. Using her fairy glow, Tink lit the way for the villainous pirates as they kidnapped both Wendy *and* her home.

Hours later, Wendy was awakened by a gentle swaying. She opened her eyes and sat up. Then she heard the sound of lapping waves and the creak of a sail.

Wendy sprang to the door and threw it open. Her eyes went wide when she found herself on the deserted deck of the *Jolly Roger*! Only then did Wendy hear the music. The elegant tinkling of a harpsichord. Drawn to the gentle sound, Wendy followed the music to the open door of Captain Hook's cabin. In the dim shadows beyond the door, she saw Captain Hook, sitting at the elegant instrument.

"Wendy Darling," said Hook as he ended his song. "You are, I trust, well?"

Wendy swallowed hard. "I feel rather frightened."

Captain Hook smiled devilishly. "Then you have heard of Hook?"

Wendy nodded once. "The only man whom Barbeque feared. And Flint himself feared Barbeque."

Hook chuckled. "A long time ago, my beauty," he purred. Then Hook gazed upon his hook and his eyes burned with crimson fire. "Before damnation . . ."

"Why do you hate him so?" Wendy asked.

"Imagine a lion in a cage, and into that cage flies a butterfly," said Hook. "If the lion was free it would pay no heed to such a creature. But the lion is not free, so the butterfly slowly drives it insane."

Hook pointed to a dining table in the corner. It was set up for two. Wendy sat down. Smee, a towel draped over his arm, emerged from the shadows and offered Wendy a drink.

"Muscat, Miss?"

The smell of the alcohol made Wendy queasy. "I am a little girl," she informed him.

Smee smiled. "Rum, then?"

"No, thank you," said Wendy.

"I am told you ran away from home," Hook remarked as he sat down at the table.

Wendy blinked in surprise. "I had never thought of it that way," she said. "I suppose I did."

"How wonderful," Hook said.

"My parents wanted me to grow up," she explained.

Hook sighed deeply. "Growing up is a barbarous business full of inconvenience and pimples."

"Grown-ups don't usually say so," Wendy replied.

"Of course not," said Hook, shaking his mane of black, oily curls. "They pretend otherwise. But not one of them is happy to be old."

Hook turned to his boatswain. "Smee, do you enjoy being this wretched ageing goat, or would you rather be young?"

Smee smiled toothlessly. "Young, Cap'n."

"Why do we grow up at all?" Wendy cried.

Hook frowned. "Somebody has to be responsible," he explained. "Grown-ups organise the world that children and pirates play in. We must thank them for that, and pity them all else. Poor dull things. Trapped by propriety, kowtowing to authority. Tormented by feelings . . ."

"Feelings?" Wendy repeated

"Dreadful things," Hook said. "I have been the victim of feelings all my life. Rage, principally. It has driven me to acts so unspeakable I scarcely recognise myself. What could be worse than rage?"

"Love," Wendy said softly.

Hook nodded. "Aye, love. That *is* worse."

"Things were simpler when I was younger," admitted Wendy with a sigh.

"And then the mess starts," Hook replied. "The feelings come. Pan is so lucky to be untroubled by them. He cannot love. It is part of the riddle of his being. The solution to the riddle eludes us all."

Wendy sobbed and a tear stained her pink cheek.

"Cigar?" asked Smee, thrusting a humidor at her. Hook kicked the boatswain, and he quickly fled the Captain's quarters.

"It does not have to be this way," said Hook. "Didn't you ever want to be a pirate, my hearty? I do not kowtow, nor care what society thinks. And I have never, *never* loved."

Wendy looked up. "I once thought of calling myself Red-handed Jill," she said shyly.

Hook slammed his hook on to the table. "And a good name, too! We shall call you that if you join."

"What would my duties be?" Wendy asked, excitement growing inside her. "I could not be expected to pillage."

Hook snorted. "The modern pirate does not countenance such behaviour. Do you tell stories?"

"Stories?" Wendy said, blushing. "Actually, I have told stories about you."

"I'm touched," said Hook.

"But I could not ally myself to you against Peter Pan!" Wendy insisted.

"If you were to join me, I should forget my vendetta against Pan," Hook said seriously.

Suddenly, Wendy was suspicious. *"Why?"*

Hook jumped to his feet so fast the table shook.

"No little children love me," he roared. "I am told they play at Peter Pan, and that the strongest always chooses to be Peter. They would rather be Twin than Hook! They force the dog to be Hook. The *dog*!"

Hook sighed. "That is not how I want to be remembered," he said, softly now. "I want someone to tell the true story of Hook, the good with the bad."

Hook took Wendy by the hand and stood her up.

"A little fairy told me 'when *Wendy Darling* recounts an adventure, it is better than *having* it!'"

Captain Hook led Wendy to the door of his cabin. Outside, the entire pirate crew of the *Jolly Roger* stood before her.

"Brutes!" Hook cried, lifting Wendy's hand with his. "I give you Red-handed Jill, Storyteller!"

The pirates gathered around Wendy. Someone gave her a stool, and Wendy sat down. Eagerly, the pirates waited for her to begin. Wendy cleared her throat.

"Once upon a time," she began. "There was a girl named Wendy Darling, who found herself most impertinently surrounded by pirates!"

All the pirates listened intently as Wendy told her tale. The morning turned to noon, and then to evening, but no one moved or uttered a sound.

Even the mermaids who swam in the cove gathered around to listen to Red-handed Jill's most utterly amazing story, until the sun fell below the horizon and the moon rose high in the sky.

When her story was through, Wendy approached Captain Hook.

"Might I have time to consider your generous offer?" she asked.

Hook nodded, then bowed. He opened the door to Wendy's little house and pushed her gently inside.

"My fellows will deliver you to whence they found you," he said. Then Captain Hook lifted Wendy's hand and gently kissed it.

"What would Mother think of my becoming a pirate?" she wondered.

"Do you remember your mother?" Hook replied.

Wendy blinked, appalled at his suggestion. "Why of course I . . ." Then Wendy frowned. She could not quite remember her mother!

"Till we meet again," Hook said. He smiled as he closed the door.

When he was done, Hook returned to his cabin. He gazed into a glass medicine cabinet, where Smee had accidently trapped poor Tinker Bell.

"Don't fret my dear," Hook growled. "When Peter is dead, both you and I will be free."

Tink's eyes widened in horror. Now Peter was in danger!

Frantically, Tinker Bell beat against the glass. But no matter how hard she tried, the little fairy could not escape. Sobbing, Tinker Bell's fairy light grew dimmer and dimmer with each new wave of Hook's cruel laughter.

11

Red-handed Jill

When she awoke the next morning, Wendy ran to the door and flung it open. Outside she saw the grassy clearing where the Lost Boys built the house. Hook had kept his word.

But Wendy's thoughts were still troubled. She was particularly bothered by something Hook had said to her. She hurried to the big tree with the hole in it that led to Peter Pan's underground lair.

Wendy found her brothers, John and Michael, eating breakfast with the Lost Boys at a long wooden table.

"John," said Wendy, gazing into her brother's eyes. "What is your father's name?"

"My father's name?" he said, puzzled by the question. "Peter!"

Wendy turned to her youngest brother. "Michael," she demanded. "Who is your mother?"

Michael smiled at her. "You are my mother, Wendy."

Wendy looked at all of the Lost Boys. "And how long a time have we been here?" she asked.

"'Tis hard to say," said Slightly. "What time is it?"

Just then Peter Pan arrived. He walked over to Wendy, his face serious.

"There is a new pirate aboard the *Jolly Roger*," he declared. "The mermaids say she is called Redhanded Jill."

Instantly, the Lost Boys jumped to their feet and grabbed their weapons.

"Redhanded Jill!" cried Tootles. "She sounds quite fearsome."

But Peter scoffed. "She is just a storyteller."

"Just a storyteller!" Wendy cried indignantly. "Red-handed Jill may be a brave swordsman."

Peter drew his own sword and waved it. "Brave or not, I shall run her through!" he boldly declared.

"Then arm yourself, Peter Pan," said Wendy, drawing a sword of her own. "For *I* am Redhanded Jill!"

There were shocked gasps all around.

"Mother!" cried Tootles plaintively.

"Wendy!" John said.

"'Tis true, John," said Wendy defiantly. "Your sister has been invited to piracy!"

Peter Pan glared angrily at Wendy.

"But, Mother," Curly wailed. "Hook is a fiend."

"On the contrary," Wendy replied. "I find Captain Hook to be a man of *feeling*." Then she glared at Peter, who responded to her words by thrusting his sword under her chin.

"Mother and Father are fighting again," said Tootles with a sigh.

"Sir," said Wendy, staring hard at Peter. "You are both ungallant and deficient."

Peter sneered. "How am I deficient?"

Wendy tossed her hair back. "You are *nothing* but a boy."

Peter lowered his sword.

Michael said, "Are you really to be a pirate, Mother?"

"No," said Wendy, her eyes still on Peter. "We are going home."

"Home?" gasped Michael.

"Leave Neverland?" said John, aghast.

"We must," Wendy declared. "We have forgotten our parents. We must leave at once. Before we in turn are forgotten."

The Lost Boys begged Wendy to stay, but she ignored them.

"Peter, stop her!" cried First Twin.

Wendy waited for Peter to reply. His answer surprised her.

"If you wish it," he said. Peter's voice was cold and distant.

The Lost Boys were stunned, but before they could make an outcry, Peter climbed a tree and escaped the underground lair.

Outside, unseen by the others, Peter took to the sky. He felt like screaming! He didn't want Wendy to leave, but he didn't know how to stop her.

Peter slowed his flight until he was merely floating. Hanging in the air over the green, green valley, Peter Pan fought back tears . . .

Under the ground, the Lost Boys watched in mounting panic as Wendy and her brothers prepared to leave.

"Please don't leave us," sobbed Tootles.

Wendy turned to the boys and her heart melted. "If you were to come with me I feel almost sure I could get my mother and father to adopt you," she told them.

Slightly scratched his dirty head. "But won't they think us rather a handful?"

"Oh, no," Wendy replied. "It will only mean having a few beds in the drawing room. They can be hidden behind screens at tea-time."

The Lost Boys cheered and began to gather their stuff. Suddenly Peter Pan was among them again.

"I have arranged a fairy guide to lead you back," Peter told Wendy.

"Won't you lead us?" Wendy asked. But Peter

turned away from her, and Wendy knew the answer.

The Lost Boys crowded around her now, all packed and ready to go.

"Peter isn't coming," Wendy announced.

The Lost Boys gasped.

"Not coming?" Slightly cried. "I won't go, either." He put down his bag of stuff and sat on it.

"No!" said Peter. "You all go."

No one moved.

"What are you waiting for?" he cried. "Go! I shall be here, having fun."

As if to prove it, Peter plunked himself down and began to blow on his pan pipes.

On top of a tree, a grizzled old fairy, puffing a big smelly cigar, waited to lead Wendy and company back to London and home. His golden fairy light throbbed with impatience. He wanted to get this trip over with and return swiftly to Neverland.

The leaves near the fairy's head were parted by a shiny silver claw. Captain Hook poked his head from the shadows and whispered a simple phrase in the fairy's ear.

"There's no such thing as fairies."

At the sound of those terrible words, the fairy gasped and stiffened. His fairy light dimmed, then went out. The fairy tumbled from the tree, dead.

Back at Hook's cabin aboard the *Jolly Roger*, poor Tinker Bell was frantic. The little fairy had overheard Captain Hook's evil plan for Peter, and she wanted to flitter off and warn him. But Tink was trapped inside a medicine cabinet, behind glass walls.

Just then, Hook's ugly parrot waddled into the cabin, its wooden leg clicking against the deck. With a squawk, the parrot hopped onto the table and began to feast on the remains of Hook's dinner.

Seeing her chance to escape, Tinker Bell began to make a loud tinkling sound. When the parrot heard the strange noise, it tilted its head to gaze with one eye at the medicine cabinet.

Inside, Tink waved at the bird. When the parrot saw her, Tinker Bell made a face, taunting the parrot. The bird ruffled its feathers. Then it fluttered over to the medicine cabinet and cawed angrily. Tink turned around and wiggled her bottom in the parrot's face.

The furious bird lifted the medicine cabinet's latch with its beak and pulled open the glass door. Suddenly, Tink burst free of her cage. The startled parrot reeled backwards. Seeing her chance, Tinker Bell circled the cabin and returned to kick the bird into the medicine cabinet.

In a flash she threw the latch and tinkled. The trapped parrot cawed and kicked its wooden leg against the glass.

Tinker Bell was already gone – streaking over the forest like a shooting star. She had to warn Peter Pan that he was in danger, before it was too late.

As the Lost Boys prepared for their journey, Peter and Wendy found themselves alone. Wendy plucked a tulip and poured dew that had gathered in a leaf into the flower bud. She laid the cup on a stump close to Peter.

"Don't forget your medicine," she said.

Peter lowered his pipes but said nothing.

"You will be awfully lonely in the evenings, Peter," Wendy said with a frown.

"I shall have Tink!" Peter declared. Then he remembered he had banished Tinker Bell. "Oh. It doesn't matter," he said, with a wave of his hand.

Peter sprawled across his bed and turned his back on Wendy. She reached out for him, but then she pulled her hand back. Eyes downcast, Wendy left the underground lair. Only after she was gone did Peter Pan look after her.

On the mantle, the sound of the clock tick-ticking broke the lonely silence of Peter Pan's empty lair.

As Wendy emerged from the tree, rough hands forced a gag over her mouth. She tried to scream, but only a whimper came out. Terrified, Wendy saw that her kidnappers were Captain Hook and his pirate crew.

"Do not fret, my dear," Hook hissed. "I will free us both."

Wendy watched in horror as Captain Hook

climbed through the opening in the tree. She struggled helplessly as she and the Lost Boys were carried away by the cutthroat pirate band.

In his home underground, Peter lay asleep in his hammock. Hook could see Pan clearly, but the hole in the tree was only large enough to admit a little girl or boy – not a grown-up pirate. Hook reached out his claw, but it stopped agonisingly short of Peter's tender neck. The pirate scowled.

Then he saw the tulip cup brimming with Wendy's medicine. From his long pirate coat, Hook drew a small glass vial. The blood-red liquid inside the tiny bottle had been made from the tears of Hook's eyes when he wept. A mixture of malice, jealousy and disappointment, the poison was instantly fatal. Gleefully, Hook poured a few drops into the tulip cup.

As Hook made his escape, Peter woke calling for Wendy. He sat up, searching for her – and for his Lost Boys.

Then Peter remembered that Wendy was gone, and so were his boys. Peter frowned. He was alone now.

His eyes fell on the cup of medicine, and Peter remembered Wendy's final words: "Don't forget your medicine."

Peter smiled, remembering. Then he lifted the cup and placed it to his lips.

12

Do You Believe in Fairies?

As Peter raised the tulip cup to his lips, he saw a bright flash. Streaking like a roman candle, Tink raced through the hole in the tree, down the roots, and into Peter's home under the ground.

In the blink of an eye, Tink shot across the room.

"Tink!" Peter cried as the fairy tried to pull the tulip cup out of his hand. "Stop it!"

Tinker Bell flitted in front of Peter's bluer-than-blue eyes, tinkling urgently.

"Poison!" Peter said with a scoff. "Why would Wendy give me poison?"

The fairy frantically tinkled, louder this time.

"Hook!" cried Peter in disbelief. "Don't be silly. How could Hook get down here?"

Once again, Peter lifted the cup to his lips. Again, Tinker Bell pushed it away. "Stop it," Peter yelled, angry now. With the back of his hand, Peter swatted Tinker Bell across the room. She landed in a pile of golden doubloons.

"I banished you for this very reason!" Peter cried. "Spitefulness."

Peter lifted the cup a third time. Then he tilted back his head and opened his mouth. In a flash, Tink darted across the room and straight into Peter Pan's wide open mouth! Quick as she could, the little fairy gulped down the poison as it passed Peter's lips.

Gagging, Peter spat Tinker Bell out of his mouth. The fairy landed on the floor, then tried to rise. But already, Hook's deadly poison was taking effect. Tink staggered, then fell.

Peter gasped in horror as he realised the truth – Tinker Bell had tried to save him. She had sacrificed her own life for his.

"Tink!" Peter cried. "Tinker Bell!"

But the fairy did not move. As Peter watched, her glow began to fade.

"No!" bellowed Peter, striking the ground with his fists. "Dear Tink! Please don't die."

The fairy rose once again, then fell back.

"Tinker Bell!" Peter said. But the fairy's light had gone out. Peter lifted her gently in his arms and carried Tinker Bell outside, into the bright sunshine. He knelt and lay the motionless fairy on a bed of soft moss. Tears ran down Peter's cheeks.

At that moment, the sun slipped behind a mass of dark, threatening clouds, and a cold wind began to blow . . .

By the time those clouds reached Pirates Cove, they were crackling with lightning and roaring with thunder. And the cold wind had become a gale.

"Cap'n!" Smee cried in alarm. "Look at the sky! The water!"

Hook emerged from his cabin, polishing his silvery claw with a ragged cloth. He glanced at Wendy, who was tied to the main mast. Then

Hook turned his eye on the Lost Boys, who were lashed to the gunwales. Then he scanned the water. The sea was dark and choppy, and chunks of ice bobbed up and down on the rising waves.

"Ya done it, Cap'n," Smee said with a toothless grin. "Pan must be dead."

At that moment, the sky opened and sleet and snow began to fall. Captain Hook hopped on the railing and turned to face his crew.

"Ship's company, hats off!" Hook commanded. "A moment of silence for our fallen enemy, Peter Pan."

The cut-throat crew removed their hats and bowed their heads solemnly. A few seconds passed, then Hook spoke.

"Let the revelry begin! We sail at dawn."

Lightning crackled in the angry sky, and the waves crashed higher around them. As Wendy and the Lost Boys shivered, the pirates cheered and threw their ragged hats into the air.

Back in the forest, Peter Pan sobbed over the still form of Tinker Bell. Around him trees swayed, and winds howled. The sky grew darker, and snow fell hard.

"Please, Tink! Don't leave me."

But the little fairy did not move.

As snow began to blanket the mossy bed she lay on, Peter Pan turned his eyes to the darkened heavens and spoke the most magical words he knew –

"I do believe in fairies. I do. I do . . ."

A peal of thunder challenged him, but Peter lifted his voice.

"I do believe in fairies. I do! I do!"

Wind and snow lashed his face, but Peter would not be halted. Yelling at the boiling clouds, he cried once more –

"I DO BELIEVE IN FAIRIES! I DO! I DO!"

Something happened just then. Something strange. Something magical. Everyone who lived in Neverland felt it. And everyone in the world, young and old, everyone who had ever dreamed of Neverland felt it, too.

The force of Peter's powerful wish carried to the four corners of the Earth, echoing through space, and trickling down to be taken up by all those who were able to hear it in their hearts.

On the deck of the *Jolly Roger*, there was laughter and celebration. Pan was dead, and even Captain Hook wore a wide, toothy grin.

Smee, Cecco, Cookson, and another pirate called Alsatian Fogarty were drinking ale and swapping sea stories and sentimental reminiscences.

"Remember when Pan stole me hat an' give it to the Neverbird for a nest?" chortled Cecco.

Cookson, Fogarty and Smee all laughed heartily.

"Or the day Pan thought our poisoned cake was a bomb an' dropped it on Smee's head!" said Cookson. "Remember Smee?"

The boatswain laughed and nodded. But when he opened his mouth, something strange came out of it.

"I do!" said Smee. "I do believe in fairies, I do, I do!"

"What?" Cecco cried.

The pirates were surprised. None more than

Smee himself. A look of shock and puzzlement crossed his grizzled face.

"Nuttin'," said Smee.

Fogarty got into Smee's face. "Did ya jus say somethin' about fairies?" he demanded.

"Why would I be sayin' anythin' about fairies!" Smee shot back, furious now. "Or believin' in fairies, I do, I do, I do!"

The other pirates gaped at Smee, who clapped his hand over his mouth. From the mast, Wendy watched the pirates, then turned to face her brothers. They nodded. So did the Lost Boys. Clearly, *something* was up.

"I do believe in fairies," said Wendy in a loud voice. "I do, I do!"

"I do believe in fairies," said Michael and John. "I do, I do!"

"I do believe in fairies! I do, I do," Wendy, Michael and John repeated, the Lost Boys joining in the chant.

"Stop that gab!" Fogarty cried, drawing his blade. "Or I'll run ya through I do believe in fairies, I do, I do, I do!"

Alsatian Fogarty's eyes widened in horror. Wendy, her brothers, and the Lost Boys continued to chant.

The wind increased with the snow. Waves whipped up, tossing the *Jolly Roger* like a toy in a child's bathtub. The ship rolled to port, and then to starboard. Pirates were tossed helplessly to the deck.

"I duh be-weeve im fairwes, I duh, I duh," cried Smee, the words muffled by his hands, still clapped over his mouth.

"Awwwwwkkkkk!" crowed the ugly parrot. "Fairies! Believe! I do! I do! I do!"

Hearing the chant, the grin Hook wore turned to a sneer. The colour melted from his face. Angrily, he dug his claw into the rail.

Over London – a world away – the skies had darkened. Clouds blotted out the sun. Lightning flashed. Thunder rumbled and shook the windows of all the city's houses, factories and shops.

But not everyone saw the lightning, or heard the thunder. Poor Mrs Darling had fallen into a troubled sleep as she sat in her rocking chair, waiting by the open window of the nursery, waiting for her lost children to return. And in her sleep, she dreamed. And in that dreaming, she spoke –

"I do believe in fairies," Mrs Darling whispered. "I do, I do . . ."

She was not alone in speaking this strange and magical phrase. The children of London, dreaming in their beds, took up the chant, too.

"I do believe in fairies. I do, I do . . ."

And elsewhere, at a sumptuous wedding in a vast London cathedral, the Bride turned to the Groom and said, "I do." The Groom smiled back at his beloved and replied, "I do."

Then the vicar, enthralled by the joy before him, found himself saying, "Believe in fairies."

Some in the pews gasped, but the Bride and Groom in their waking dream took up the chant. "I do, I do!" they said as one.

Meanwhile, at the Fidelity Bank and Assurance Company, Sir Edward Quiller-Couch was conducting a meeting. Sitting at a long oak table, surrounded by his managers, he stared at poor Mr Darling.

"I cannot believe my eyes!" Sir Edward sputtered. "A clerk in the most esteemed financial house in London residing in a . . . a . . . dog hotel!"

"A *kennel*," the manager sitting on his right corrected him.

At the opposite end of the table sat Mr Darling, head bowed. Next to his chair sat Nana's kennel. Since the night Nana tried to warn him of the danger to his children, Mr Darling had lived in that kennel. It was punishment, self-inflicted, for being so wrong not to trust Nana with the lives and well-being of Wendy, John and little Michael.

"Explain yourself, man," Sir Edward demanded.

Mr Darling opened his mouth to speak, but the words that came out of his mouth were most unexpected.

"I do believe in fairies," said Mr Darling. "I do, I do!"

To his surprise, it felt good to say those words. Mr Darling smiled for the first time since his children ran away.

"I do believe in fairies," he said in a loud, clear voice. "I do, I do!"

The managers exchanged startled glances. Sir Edward shifted uncomfortably in his chair. Something about Mr Darling's strange words had touched a part of his heart that had not been reached in a very long time.

"I DO BELIEVE IN FAIRIES! I DO, I DO!" Mr Darling cried, jumping to his feet. To the amazement of all, the bank managers took up the chant.

"We do believe in fairies!" they chanted. "We do, we do!"

Even sour Aunt Millicent, singing in her bath, could recall a time long ago when she had dreamed of Neverland.

"I do believe in fairies!" she sang. "I do, I do!"

Now all of London was chanting that powerful, mystical phrase. The words, whispered in sleep, cried out in dreams, or spoken for no-one-knew-why, lifted high on the wind and soared back to Neverland.

13

Hook or Me This Time

In the forest of Neverland, Peter blinked at Tinker Bell. Her tiny body, which had been so cold and dim, now began to pulse with the faintest glow.

"I do believe in fairies! I do, I do . . ."

The wind that howled around them sounded magically like voices. Thousands of them. Tens of thousands. Their whisperings, carried by the wind, echoed through trees and shook the snowy blanket from the leaves.

"I do believe in fairies! I do! I do!"

Tink's light grew stronger, pulsing brighter

with each passing minute. Finally she twitched, and her wings began to flutter.

"I do believe in fairies! I do! I do!" shouted Peter into the heavens.

When he looked down again, Tinker Bell's glow was as bright as it ever was. Slowly, the fairy opened her eyes.

"You're alive! You're alive!" cried Peter Pan. "Oh, Tink! You're alive."

The skies above Pirates Cove were calm again. The lightning, the thunder and the snow vanished as quickly as they had come. The deck of the *Jolly Roger* became steady as the waves became glass.

Finally, the chanting died away, and the pirates shook their heads as if awakening from a trance.

Wendy and the Lost Boys stopped chanting, too. As the sun broke through the clouds and warmed their cheeks, the children shook the snow from their hair.

Captain Hook's face was as pale as the snow that had fallen. His eyes were as red as the blood he liked to spill.

"He's alive," the pirate captain growled. Hook threw his eyes skyward, and shook his iron claw at the heavens.

"HE'S ALIVE!" Hook bellowed, so loudly that the main sails shook and the pirates quaked in their boots.

"Why is he?" roared Hook. "*Where* is he?"

With crimson fire still burning in his eyes, Hook charged Wendy. Still lashed to the mast, Wendy gasped and struggled helplessly against the ropes. Then she felt the cold metal of Hook's claw against her throat, and she froze stiff as a statue.

"I shall have one more story before ye die. The story of Peter Pan," said Hook. "Once upon a time . . ." he prompted.

Wendy, terrified, opened her trembling lips. "Once . . . upon a time . . ." she whispered.

Smee grew excited. He grabbed the arm of Cookson and shushed the others. "Brutes!" he cried. "Red-handed Jill is tellin' a story."

The pirates gathered around her, but all Wendy could see were Hook's red eyes burning into her soul.

". . . There was a boy named Peter Pan who decided not to grow up," Wendy continued. "So he flew away to the Neverland, where the pirates are—"

"Was one o' the pirates called Noodler?" Noodler interrupted.

"Yes," said Wendy with a nod.

"Am I in a story?" said Noodler, amazed. "Cap'n, I am in a story!"

Hook drew his pistol and shot Noodler. Then he turned back to Wendy, and dug his claw just a little bit deeper into her throat. Wendy stifled a cry.

"What fun Peter must have had," prompted Hook.

"Yes," whispered Wendy. "But he was rather lonely."

"Lonely?" said Hook.

"There was no one to tell stories," Wendy explained.

Hook sighed and nodded. "He needed a Wendy."

Alsatian Fogarty sighed, too. "I need a Wendy!" he said. Those were Fogarty's last words, for Hook shot him, too!

"'Tis very excitin'!" Smee exclaimed. "Two dead already!"

"Why a Wendy?" Hook growled. "And not a Phoebe, or a Jane? What makes Wendy the nicer?"

"He liked my stories," Wendy replied.

"What stories?" Hook asked, withdrawing the claw from her neck.

Wendy thought about it. "Cinderella," she said. "And Snow White and Sleeping Beauty."

"Love stories!" roared Hook.

But Wendy shook her head. "Adventures!" she cried. "In which good triumphs over evil."

Hook raised his eyebrow. "They all end with a kiss," he said. Then the pirate studied Wendy's face, her mouth.

"A kiss," Hook said thoughtfully, rubbing his chin as if he were trying to figure something out. "He needed a Wendy. With a kiss . . ."

Suddenly Hook understood.

"He *does* feel," Hook said to Wendy. "He feels about *you*."

Captain Hook giggled with glee, then pressed

the claw into Wendy's throat again. "After the stories, what then?"

"He taught me to fly," said Wendy.

Hook blinked. "How?"

"You just think happy thoughts, and they lift you into the air," said Wendy, smiling at the memory.

"Alas," sighed Hook. "I *have* no happy thoughts."

"That brings you down," said Wendy.

Hook didn't like Wendy's answer, so he dug his claw just a little deeper.

"Fairy dust!" Wendy cried. "You need the fairy dust."

"And what of Pan?" Hook said ominously. "Will unhappy thoughts bring him down?"

"He has no unhappy thoughts," Wendy cried.

Hook chuckled. "What if his Wendy walks the plank?"

Captain Hook waved his good hand, and the pirates untied Wendy and set up the plank. As the pirates prepared to send Wendy to her doom, Captain Hook danced and sang and cavorted like a madman.

"Yo ho, yo ho, the pirate life," he sang. "The flag of skull and bones! A merry day for she walks the plank, and hey for Davy Jones!"

As the pirates tied Wendy's hands behind her back, and blindfolded the girl with a silken cloth, they took up Hook's song.

"Avast, belay, ye curse yer God," they sang, "An' bravely out ya go."

Smee plunked Wendy down on the narrow wooden plank that hung over the water. Prodded by Hook's curved cutlass, Wendy stepped onto the narrow board. The hard, splintery wood scratched her bare feet. Captain Hook bent low and whispered into Wendy's ear.

"An' if ye part before me—" Hook kissed her cheek. "– Fear not, we meet below!"

With that, Captain Hook shoved Wendy out over the black water. Still lashed to the gunwales, the Lost Boys squealed in fright. The *Jolly Roger* rocked, and Wendy tottered on the very edge of the long plank.

Struggling, she regained her balance at the very last possible moment. Spinning on her toes, Wendy turned her back on the water to face Hook again. The captain snarled and prodded her again.

Just then, everyone heard a familiar, ominous ticking of a clock. The crocodile!

"Oh, the irony," Captain Hook declared. "It comes for Hook and gets a story."

With that, Hook stomped on the plank until Wendy toppled off the end!

The pirates rushed to the rail, listening for Wendy's screams. But there was only silence.

"Nothing," said Smee.

Hook grinned. "The brute has swallowed her whole."

Just then, the ticking sound seemed to move from one side of the *Jolly Roger* to the other. "Port side!" Smee cried.

The pirates rushed headlong to the opposite side of the ship. The cutthroats stared into the water, but it was too dark to see anything below the surface. Still the ticking persisted.

"It looks for more, Cap'n!" said Smee.

"Then give it more!" Hook cried, pointing at the Lost Boys. "All eight courses! Move the plank."

The pirates crossed the deck and grabbed the plank. Soon it was set up again, on the port side. Hook raised his cutlass and stalked the helpless Lost Boys.

"Mercy, mercy!" Slightly pleaded.

"Silence, spewing spawn! I'll show you the road to dusty death," Hook roared.

But it was Michael's rope Hook cut. Then he hooked the boy's collar with his claw and hoisted Michael in the air. The boy squealed and kicked his legs as Hook carried him to the plank.

"A banquet of children," Hook chuckled. "There is something grand in the idea."

"Cap'n!" yelled Smee, pointing to the water. "It moves again!"

This time the ticking sound seemed to go around the *Jolly Roger* once and then fade. The pirates listened, ears straining.

Then the sound! This time high up in the mast.

"Cap'n! It flies," said Smee.

Hook paled. "It is not possible."

Another pirate pointed to a shadow in the sails. "The brute has wings!" he howled fearfully.

Hook lifted his eyes. He saw it, too. The silhouette of a large figure was framed by the main sail.

Hook cursed. "And all this time it was a dragon. Into the rigging with ye! Hunt it down!"

"No, Cap'n, no!" Smee cried. He was terrified of dragons.

Hook shook his claw under Smee's nose. "Into the rigging or I'll cast anchor in you!"

Up the rigging climbed the pirates, while Hook aimed his pistol into the sails where the strange shadow still moved.

Suddenly there was a scream. A pirate dropped from the rigging and plunged headfirst into the dark water.

"What was that?" gasped Hook.

"One," said Slightly.

Clinging to the mast with one hand, Smee drew his pistol as a shadow glided across the highest sail. He pulled the trigger. The gun went off in a blast of fire and smoke and another pirate plunged into the sea.

"Two," said Slightly.

A scream rang out. A pirate, arms flapping, hit the water head first.

"Three," said Slightly.

Pirate Bill Jukes closed in on the shadow. He raised his dagger to plunge it into the creature's heart. But at that moment the sail blew aside, just as Bill Jukes swung his blade. On the way down, the pirate saw the creature they had been battling.

It was Tinker Bell, holding a clock and flitting among the masts. Her fairy glow had created the strange shapes silhouetted by the sail.

"Four," said Slightly as Jukes slammed to the deck at Captain Hook's feet. The pirate whirled about and saw Peter Pan standing behind him, Wendy in his arms!

"So, Pan. This is all your doing," Hook snarled.

Peter Pan nodded and drew his sword. "Aye James Hook, it is all my doing."

Hook raised his own blade.

"Proud and insolent youth," cried Hook. "Prepare to meet thy doom."

Peter frowned, his bluer-than-blue eyes burning with determination.

"Dark and sinister man, have at thee!" yelled Peter.

With a crash of metal and a flash of sparks, their blades met.

It was Hook or Peter now!

14

Journey's End

A splendid battle began on the deck of the *Jolly Roger*. Peter Pan had freed the Lost Boys from their bonds. Now armed, they fought the pirates in a desperate fight of good against evil.

"Six . . . Seven," Slightly cried, as more pirates fell to the battle skills of the Lost Boys.

Meanwhile, Peter and Hook thrust, parried, lunged and riposted with dazzling speed. So evenly matched were they that each thrust was blocked, each lunge dodged.

When things began to look bad for the crew of the *Jolly Roger*, some of the pirates began to think of retreating. One of them was Smee, who made his way into Captain Hook's cabin to help himself to some of the pirate booty.

As Michael sent another pirate overboard, he turned to confront Smee, who was now sneaking out of Hook's quarters, pockets stuffed with jewels.

"Please, lad, let me live," Smee begged as he dropped to his knees. "I'll turn over a new leaf, I swear. I'll spend the rest of me days doin' good!"

Michael placed the tip of his sword at Smee's neck. "You will join a nunnery," the boy commanded.

Smee nodded vigorously. "A nunnery! Good idea. Sister Mary Smee, here I come!"

The pirate rose to leave, but Michael cleared his throat. Sighing, Smee emptied his pockets, handing over all of the jewels to Michael. Then he leaped over the rail and into the water.

On the great ship's bowsprit, Peter Pan had cornered Captain Hook. They traded sword blows until, with a deft stroke, Hook whipped the sword from Peter's hand.

Hook lunged for the kill. Too late! Peter was

airborn now. Swooping low, he scooped up his blade from the deck and again soared out of Hook's reach. The pirate roared with frustration.

Then Hook spied Tinker Bell, tormenting the pirate Quang Lee. As Tink pulled on the man's ponytail, then sent him over the side, Hook recalled Wendy's tale, and the magical, aerodynamic properties of fairy dust.

With a quick lunge, Hook seized Tink and shook the fairy over his head. A gleaming shower of golden fairy dust settled in the pirate's long, curly hair. With a roar of triumph, Hook took flight!

"It's Hook!" the mad captain cried. "He flies! And he likes it!"

Peter dived out of the sky. Hook soared upwards to meet him. Their swords met far above the *Jolly Roger*'s deck. In a flash, Hook beat Peter back, forcing the boy against the mast. His back to the wall, Peter fought desperately.

"I know who you are," hissed Captain Hook.

Peter kicked at Hook, forcing the pirate backwards.

"I'm youth! I'm joy!" cried Peter. "I'm a little bird broken out of the egg."

"No!" Hook shot back. "You are a tragedy."

"Me? Tragic?" Peter scoffed.

Hook's eyes looked below, to the deck where Wendy and John battled pirates, back-to-back.

"She was leaving you, Pan," Hook cried. "Your Wendy was *leaving*. And why should she stay? What have you to offer? You are incomplete. Not whole."

Peter's eyes flashed angrily. He slashed at Hook, then ducked as Hook replied in kind.

"She would rather grow up than stay with you," taunted Hook.

Peter struck again. Their blades crashed together and sparks flew. Hook could see the suffering in Peter Pan's eyes, and Hook knew he was winning.

"Bulls-eye!" Hook roared. "Welcome to pain. I knew you had it in you."

Peter cried out, waving his sword. Hook easily parried his slash.

"Let us take a peep into the future," said Hook. "What is this I see? 'Tis the fair Wendy."

As Hook spoke, their airborn duel continued. On

the deck of the pirate ship, the children had nearly won. Most of the pirates were either gone or . . . gone!

"Wendy is in her nursery, crying," said Hook.

"She will smile soon enough when I fly in," countered Peter.

"The window is shut," cried Hook.

"I'll open it," Peter replied.

"The window is barred," Hook snarled.

"I'll call out her name."

Hook grinned his evillest grin. "She cannot hear you. She cannot see you," he told Peter. "Wendy has forgotten all about you."

As they swooped and dived, the bad things Hook was saying began to churn dark thoughts in Peter Pan's mind. Suddenly Pan was having trouble staying in the air. The bad thoughts were weighing him down!

"There is another boy in your place," Hook taunted. "He is called *Father*."

Peter lunged at Hook again, and missed. He was sinking lower and lower.

"Her tears are tears of joy," Hook continued. "The joy is called *baby*."

Peter sank lower, and lower still.

"'Tis lovely," said Hook with an exaggerated sigh of contentment. "'Tis what she has wanted all along!"

Peter cried out then, and slashed blindly. Hook easily knocked the sword from his weakened grip. The weapon struck the deck with an awful clang.

Now only Captain Hook was airborn. He thrust the tip of his cutlass against Peter Pan's neck as the boy's feet touched the deck. Hook placed his boot on Peter's chest and kicked. Peter slammed against the main mast. Hook loomed over Peter now, his claw raised for the final blow.

"You die alone and unloved, Peter Pan," said Hook. "Just like me."

As he spoke, Hook's eyes glowed eerily, his pupils dwindled to dazzling red points of fire.

Suddenly, Wendy leapt forward and seized Hook's claw. The pirate shook her off and she fell to the deck.

"Silence all!" Hook bellowed. "Silence for a Wendy's farewell."

Wendy threw herself between Hook and Peter. Tears staining her cheeks, she spoke.

"Peter. I am sorry. I must grow up," she sobbed. "But this is yours."

She leaned towards Peter, but Hook's claw thrust out to touch her chin.

Carefully, Wendy opened her hand and showed the object to Hook. "'Tis just a thimble," she said softly.

Hook roared with laughter. "How like a girl!" he cried. Then, bowing, Hook stepped back.

"By all means, my beauty," he purred. "Give Peter Pan your precious thimble!"

Wendy leaned against Peter's chest. "This belongs to you and always will," she whispered.

Then she kissed Peter on the cheek. John and Michael, who watched with the rest of the Lost Boys, gasped.

"That was no thimble," said John.

"That was a hidden kiss," said Michael.

"Stand back, lads," said Slightly, pushing Lost Boys. "'Tis a powerful thing."

Wendy pulled away from Peter. Then she

blushed the most perfect, perfect pink. More incredibly, Peter Pan was blushing, too!

"Pan," Hook hissed in amazement. "You're . . . pink!"

Tinker Bell, because she was a fairy and wise about magical things, decided it was time to take cover!

The Lost Boys were rocked off their feet as the entire ship shuddered. A low, deep rumbling shook the vessel. The main mast snapped and plunged into the dark sea. Cracks appeared on the wooden deck under Peter Pan's feet.

Suddenly a tremendous force, invisible but powerful nonetheless, blasted from Peter Pan. The power of it blew Hook backwards, and the Lost Boys, too.

With a tremendous flash, Peter exploded into the sky, spinning madly. Then he gripped the sail and did a somersault, crowing triumphantly. Finally, he released the sail and dived towards his sword, which was still sitting on the deck.

Hook staggered to his feet. He hardly had time to raise his own sword before Peter was upon him.

Their swords rang as they clashed. Once again, Hook took to the sky. Pan and Hook battled high above the dark waters of Pirates Cove.

"Hook!" Peter cried, bold and defiant now. "I may not be perfect. On the other hand, I may . . . But you are wrong about *one* thing."

Peter Pan stole a glance at Wendy, who smiled at him.

"*I am loved*!" Peter said with absolute certainty. "And always will be."

"No," Hook bellowed. "I have *won*."

Peter beat at Hook with a sword, driving him down. "You are old!" said Peter.

"I have won!" Hook replied even as he sank.

"And alone," said Peter.

"I. . . have . . . won," Hook gasped.

But he sank lower still for his head was now filled with bad and terrible feelings. And those feelings were weighing him down like an anchor in the drink.

"You are done for!" said Peter.

Only then did Captain Hook hear the sound of a ticking clock. He looked down and saw that his duel with Peter Pan took him far away from the *Jolly Roger*. As Hook's feet touched the water, the jaws of the hungry crocodile opened to receive him.

Hook trod air, trying to gain altitude. But still he sank. Finally, he tried to think happy thoughts.

"Ripping! Murder! Stabbing! Torture!" Hook cried. But it did him no good, for the Lost Boys had taken up Peter Pan's chant.

"Old. Alone. Done-for! Old. Alone. Done-for!" they chanted.

"Killing! Choking! Lawyers! Dentists!" howled Hook as the crocodile's toothy mouth opened wider.

As the crocodile's jaws closed on Captain Hook's legs, the pirate surrendered and began to chant the words that would free him forever.

"Old. Alone. Done-for," he gasped, letting the thoughts pull him under for good.

The crocodile leapt from the water and grabbed the pirate's waist.

"The end!" whimpered Hook as the crocodile swallowed him whole. The mighty jaws snapped closed and the water churned as if it were boiling. Then the sea grew calm.

Suddenly, the crocodile's snout poked out of the water and the reptile spat. Captain Hook's claw landed at the feet of the Lost Boys, who watched the pirate's demise in stunned silence.

When they saw Hook's hook, everyone began to cheer. Peter Pan landed on the deck next to Wendy and took her hand. Together, they danced.

"I am loved, loved, loved, loved, loved!" sang Peter. Then he turned and faced his band of Lost Boys. "Ready to cast off?" he asked them.

"Ship is secure," John replied, saluting smartly.

"Then anchors away, lads!" Peter commanded. "East by southeast!"

A powerful wind billowed the sails and the ship lurched forward. Wendy watched, awestruck, as a thousand fairies descended from the sky to light the mast and sails with a magical fairy glow.

To the amazement of everyone save Peter Pan, the *Jolly Roger* lifted out of the water and soared into the sky!

Entering the clouds, the ship surged ahead, its

bow cutting through the wispy vapours. On either side of the vessel, seagulls kept pace as if they were dolphins.

Wendy, her face glowing with happiness, turned to Peter. "Where are we bound, Captain?" she asked.

"For the mainland, Miss," Peter said, his voice without cheer. "For journey's end . . ."

15

The Return Home

That night, the clouds over London parted, and a pirate ship in full sail descended from the sky. Down, down the *Jolly Roger* floated, until the street lights of London illuminated the barnacles clinging to her hull.

Wisely, the fairies dimmed their magical glow, so as not to be seen by the general population. Then the ship drew alongside a tall church steeple and dropped anchor.

Inside the Darling nursery, Mrs Darling was still waiting in her chair by the open window. Waiting for her children's return, though she was losing hope of ever seeing Wendy, John, and little Michael ever again. As Mrs Darling dozed, Nana slept at her feet, waiting right along with her, paws crossed, ears down, big furry head on the nursery floor.

Unnoticed by either, a gentle breeze stirred the long sheer curtains. Three shadows, silent as ghosts, floated through the open window.

"Mother." John signed, remembering.

"Nana," said Michael, remembering.

Wendy gazed with concern at her mother's face. She seemed so sad. "Let us break it to her gently," Wendy whispered. Her brother nodded.

Quiet as mice, the children slipped between their sheets and closed their eyes. To see them now, one might believe they had never vanished so mysteriously or left their warm, cosy beds.

Mrs Darling suddenly woke, her eyes fluttering open. By her side, Nana yawned and stretched. Mrs Darling stroked the dog's head.

"Oh, Nana," she said. "I dreamed my dear ones had come back."

Mrs Darling and Nana gazed at the three little

beds. Three little lumps were buried under blankets – one in each bed. But Mrs Darling was so used to her children being gone, their beds empty, that she did not seem to notice the change.

"I dreamed they were sleeping in their beds," she told Nana. "But they will never come back." Then she breathed the saddest of sighs.

Downstairs, the door opened. Aunt Millicent called up to tell Mrs Darling that Mr Darling was home from his job at the bank.

Glancing once more at the children's beds, Mrs Darling rose and left the nursery. Nana followed at her heels.

After Mrs Darling had left, the children sat up in their beds, truly perplexed. Did Mother not see them? Did Nana not smell them?

On the stairs, Mrs Darling met Mr Darling.

"Hullo, dearest," said Mrs Darling. "What sort of day . . ." Suddenly Mrs Darling's mouth snapped shut and her eyes grew wide. Without a word, Mrs Darling turned and raced up the stairs again.

Mr Darling scratched his head in bewilderment

at his wife's behaviour. Aunt Millicent was about to follow Mrs Darling up to the nursery when she heard a knock at the front door. Aunt Millicent scurried off to answer it.

When Mrs Darling burst into the nursery, she found Wendy, John, and Michael standing there waiting for her.

"Hullo, Mother," said John. "It really *is* us."

Mrs Darling, tears of joy in her bright eyes, fell to her knees and threw open her arms. The children rushed to embrace her. "George! George! Come quickly," Mrs Darling called.

Mr Darling rushed into the nursery.

"We are back, Father!" said Michael. "Did you miss us?"

"You are back . . . You are back! You are back!" Mr Darling cried, hugging them all at once.

The nursery door opened once again. In came Aunt Millicent, the Lost Boys tramping into the room behind her. The boys removed their hats, polite-like, and brushed the hair from their eyes. But their outlandish pirate clothes and dirty hands and faces made them unfit for polite company.

"The silliest thing," Aunt Millicent began. "These young gentlemen say—"

Then Aunt Millicent saw the children. She gasped. "My goodness! You are back," she cried. "You are back! You are back!" Aunt Millicent danced around the room with joy.

Wendy, who had grown quite emotional during the reunion with her mother, wiped a tear from her cheek. She crossed the room and took Nibs' hand.

"Father, Mother. I would like to introduce the Lost Boys. May I keep them?" she pleaded.

"I must say, Wendy!" Mr Darling exclaimed. "You don't do things by halves."

The Lost Boys shifted on their feet. Clutching their ragged hats in their dirty hands, they waited expectantly for Mr Darling's answer.

Mr Darling sighed. "The expense . . ."

"Would this help, Father?" Michael asked. He set a handful of precious gems, sparking jewels, and gold coins upon his bed – Smee's booty, stolen from Captain Hook's cabin.

Mr Darling stared at the King's ransom Michael had given them and smiled.

"Welcome to the family, boys!" Mr Darling declared.

The Lost Boys rushed into the welcoming arms of their new mother and father. Mr and Mrs Darling held them tightly until the boys felt lost no more.

Then, a noise on the steps made them all turn. Slightly burst into the room, late as usual. He saw the happy family and his face fell. Slightly's shoulders slumped, and he began to cry.

"What is the matter, child?" Aunt Millicent said, laying a tender hand on his quaking shoulder.

"I couldn't find the house," Slightly sobbed. "And now everyone has a mother except me."

Slightly's tale was so sad that even Aunt Millicent's prim and proper heart was melted.

"Is your name Slightly?" Aunt Millicent asked.

Slightly's face brightened. "Yes," he replied.

"Then I am your mother," Aunt Millicent said.

"How do you know?" asked Slightly, more than slightly bewildered.

Aunt Millicent smiled a wise smile. "I feel it in my bones," said she.

Slightly threw his arms around Aunt Millicent. "Mother!" he cried, brushing away a tear.

Nana barked happily. She would have plenty of nursemaid work now! But she was delighted to have the children back — and already she loved the Lost Boys!

There could not have been a lovelier sight to view. But there was none to witness it except a strange boy who was staring through the window. A boy who would never grow up.

Peter Pan had delights innumerable that other children would never know, but he was looking at the one joy from which he would be forever barred.

"To live would be an awfully big adventure," Peter Pan said.

As Peter turned to go, Wendy saw him floating just beyond the billowing curtains.

"Peter!" she called, rushing to the window. "You won't forget me, will you?"

"Me? Forget?" said Peter. He smiled, and his golden hair was tossed by the breeze. Wendy suddenly frowned.

"If another little girl . . . if one younger than I,"

Wendy began. But she could not go on. "Oh, Peter," Wendy said at last. "I wish I could take you in my arms and . . ."

Peter darted backwards, out of reach.

"Yes," he said. "I know."

Peter spun gracefully in the air, and his eyes turned to gaze into the starry sky.

"Will you ever come back?" Wendy called.

Peter turned and smiled at her over his shoulder. "To hear stories about me!" he said gleefully.

And then Peter Pan was gone.

Suddenly, Wendy was filled with a terrible, sweet longing. Then she turned from the window and saw the happiness in the family around her, and her heart was filled with joy.

"And anyway," Wendy quietly told herself. "Peter will return. I am sure to see him again very soon indeed."

But Wendy was not to see Peter Pan again. Not for a long, long time.

Years and years later, in the very same nursery where Wendy and her brothers once played, a mother was telling a story to her seven-year-old daughter.

The girl had long brown hair and big, bright eyes, just like Wendy Darling. And, like Wendy, she loved stories so much that she'd made up a few of her very own.

When Mother finished the bedtime story, the girl said goodnight and snuggled under her blankets.

"Good night, dear one," Mother said as she kissed her daughter's cheek. Then, by the light of the fireplace, the mother sat down on the floor to sew.

Behind her, the window opened and the curtains billowed. A figure floated through the window and settled on the floor near the bed.

"Wendy," the figure whispered to the sleeping girl. "I have come for you."

The child in the bed did not stir. "Wendy?" said Peter, looming over the little girl.

But it was the child's mother who spoke. "Hello, Peter," she said softly.

Peter Pan turned and saw the woman by the

fire. "There you are," he said. Then he pointed to the child in bed. "Is it John?"

"No," said Wendy. "John is not here now."

"Then is it Michael?"

Wendy shook her head. "Michael is gone, too."

"Is it a new one?" asked Peter.

"Yes," Wendy replied. Then she rose. "I cannot come with you, Peter," she said sadly. "I have forgotten how to fly."

Peter smiled. "I'll soon teach you again."

Wendy returned Peter's smile, but it was a wet-eyed smile all the same. "It is more than that," she told him. Then she stepped out of the shadows so Peter Pan could see her clearly.

"Oh, Wendy, you shouldn't have," Peter said when he realised that his Wendy was all grown up.

"I couldn't help it, Peter," Wendy replied. "I am a married woman now."

Peter shrank back in horror. "No, you're not!"

"And the little girl in the bed is my daughter."

"No, she is not!" Peter cried.

Peter took a step towards the sleeping girl and looked down at her. Then he sank to his knees and wept. The little girl opened her eyes and sat up, blinking.

"Boy, why are you crying?" she said.

Peter stopped sobbing and looked up. His tears were instantly forgotten.

"I am Peter Pan," he said.

"Yes, I know," the little girl said. "I have been waiting for you. I am Jane."

Peter bowed. Jane stood up on her bed and bowed in return. Then she looked to Wendy.

"May I go?" Jane pleaded. "He does need a mother."

"Yes," said Wendy softly. "I know."

There was a sudden burst of light as Tinker Bell soared through the open window. The little fairy hovered over Jane, sprinkling golden dust on the girl's head. With a squeal of delight, Jane floated off the bed.

Then Tinker Bell alighted on the window ledge and bowed low to Wendy, who bowed respectfully in return.

Finally, Peter took Jane by the hand. Together they rose in the air. After a single spin around the nursery, they soared out of the window – followed quickly by Tinker Bell.

Wendy stepped to the window, the faintest flicker of yearning in her heart. She wanted to go with them. But she couldn't. So she simply watched as Peter and Jane and Tink soared up to the heavens.

She watched them fly higher and higher until finally they seemed as bright and fleeting as shooting stars.

Peter Pan: A Storybook Based on the Hit Movie

Live the adventure with this photo-packed storybook!

ISBN: 0 743 47804 5

Peter Pan: Journey to Neverland

Discover how the Darling children prepare themselves
for their magical adventure with Peter Pan - practising
their sword-fighting skills and learning to fly!

ISBN: 0 743 49013 4

Peter Pan: Welcome to Neverland

Join the Darling children as the discover the Lost Boys'
underground hideout, meet Princess Tiger Lily, and sail
the high seas on the Jolly Roger!

ISBN: 0 743 49014 2

Peter Pan: Adventures in Neverland

WITH 8-PAGE
PHOTO INSERT

PETER PAN
the motion picture event

Adventures in Neverland

A magical retelling for younger readers with all the
adventure and excitement of J.M. Barrie's classic story.

ISBN: 0 743 47803 7

All Pocket Books are available by post from:
Simon & Schuster Cash Sales. PO Box 29
Douglas, Isle of Man IM99 1BQ
Credit cards accepted.
Please telephone 01624 836000
fax 01624 670923, Internet
http://www.bookpost.co.uk or email:
bookshop@enterprise.net for details